W9-DCA-401

The Decade of the 2000s

Catastrophic Events of the 2000s

WOODLAND HIGH SCHOOL
800 N. MOSELEY DRIVE
STOCKBRIDGE, GA 30281
(770) 389-2784

Other titles in *The Decade of the 2000s* series:

Cultural Milestones of the 2000s

Science and Technology of the 2000s

Sports and Entertainment of the 2000s

Terrorism and War of the 2000s

The Decade of the 2000s

Catastrophic Events of the 2000s

By Craig E. Blohm

ReferencePoint Press®

San Diego, CA

© 2014 ReferencePoint Press, Inc.
Printed in the United States

For more information, contact:
ReferencePoint Press, Inc.
PO Box 27779
San Diego, CA 92198
www.ReferencePointPress.com

ALL RIGHTS RESERVED.
No part of this work covered by the copyright hereon may be reproduced or used in any form or by any means—graphic, electronic, or mechanical, including photocopying, recording, taping, web distribution, or information storage retrieval systems—without the written permission of the publisher.

LIBRARY OF CONGRESS CATALOGING-IN-PUBLICATION DATA

Blohm, Craig E., 1948-
  Catastrophic events of the 2000s / by Craig E. Blohm.
    pages cm. -- (The decade of the 2000s series)
  Includes bibliographical references and index.
  ISBN-13: 978-1-60152-522-2 (hardback)
  ISBN-10: 1-60152-522-2 (hardback)
  1. Disasters--History--21st century--Juvenile literature. 2. Natural disasters--History--21st century--Juvenile literature. 3. Epidemics--History--21st century--Juvenile literature.
  4. Terrorism--History--21st century--Juvenile literature. I. Title.
  D24.B59 2013
  363.3409'0511--dc23
                                                                          2012047798

Contents

Important Events of the 2000s   **6**

Introduction
A Portent of Catastrophe   **8**

Chapter One
Our Restless Earth   **11**

Chapter Two
Killer Weather   **23**

Chapter Three
Deadly Diseases   **36**

Chapter Four
Terrorism Strikes   **50**

Chapter Five
Man-Made Catastrophes   **63**

Source Notes   **77**

**Important People: Catastrophic
Events of the 2000s**   **83**

Words of the 2000s   **85**

For Further Research   **87**

Index   **89**

Picture Credits   **95**

About the Author   **96**

Important Events of the **2000s**

2002
- Euro enters circulation
- Terrorists attack Bali tourist district in Indonesia
- Dwarf planet Quaoar is discovered
- *American Idol* debuts on Fox network
- Xbox Live revolutionizes online gaming

2004
- Hundreds of thousands die in Indian Ocean tsunami
- *Spirit* and *Opportunity* rovers explore surface of Mars
- Facebook is launched
- Hundreds die when Chechen separatists take over a school in Russia
- Palestinian leader Yasser Arafat dies
- Green Belt Movement founder Wangari Maathai of Kenya wins Nobel Peace Prize

2000
- Dire warnings of Y2K Millennium Bug fizzle
- Dot-com bubble bursts
- Israel withdraws all forces from Lebanon
- Dashboard GPS devices become widely available
- Tiger Woods becomes youngest golfer to win Grand Slam
- USS *Cole* is attacked in Yemen

| 2000 | 2001 | 2002 | 2003 | 2004 |

2001
- Terrorist attack on United States kills three thousand people
- Apple launches iPod
- World's first space tourist reaches International Space Station
- Film version of first Harry Potter book is released
- Wikipedia is launched
- United States invades Afghanistan
- Netherlands legalizes same-sex marriage

2003
- United States invades Iraq
- Space shuttle *Columbia* disintegrates on reentry
- Human genome project is completed
- Record heat wave kills tens of thousands in Europe
- China launches its first manned space mission
- WHO issues rare global health alert on SARS

2005
- YouTube is launched
- Burst levees flood New Orleans during Hurricane Katrina
- Kyoto Protocol on climate change goes into effect
- National Academies releases human embryonic stem cell research guidelines
- Earthquake devastates Kashmir
- Lance Armstrong wins seventh consecutive Tour de France (later stripped of all titles)

2008
- United States elects Barack Obama, first African American president
- Oil prices hit record high of $147 per barrel
- US Olympic swimmer Michael Phelps wins record eight gold medals
- Islamic militants attack financial district in Mumbai, India
- Universal Declaration of Human Rights marks sixtieth anniversary

2005   2006   2007   2008   2009

2006
- Pluto is demoted to dwarf planet status
- North Korea conducts its first nuclear test
- Saddam Hussein is executed in Iraq
- West African black rhino is declared extinct
- Twitter is launched
- Global warming documentary, *An Inconvenient Truth,* is released

2009
- WHO declares swine flu outbreak an international pandemic
- Mouse genome is fully sequenced
- Michael Jackson dies at his home in California
- World's tallest man-made structure is completed in Dubai
- Large Hadron Collider becomes world's highest-energy particle accelerator
- Widespread match-fixing scandal rocks European soccer

2007
- Mitchell report details rampant PED use in baseball
- Apple debuts iPhone
- Dozens killed and wounded in mass shooting at Virginia Tech
- Arctic sea ice hits record low
- Google Street View is launched
- Prime Minister Benazir Bhutto of Pakistan is assassinated
- Amazon releases its Kindle
- Great Recession, worldwide economic crisis, begins

A Portent of Catastrophe

The arrival of a new year is usually a time of joy and celebration, of putting the old behind and looking forward to a new beginning. December 31, 1999, was eagerly anticipated, for it marked not only the end of a year but also the beginning of a new century and a new millennium. The twenty-first century was making its entrance at a time of relative peace and prosperity. But while most people around the world were happily preparing for midnight parties and spectacular fireworks displays, others were fearful that the beginning of the new century would create a disaster that could bring the world to a halt.

The Millennium Bug

What these people feared began decades earlier, when computers were just beginning to become useful tools for business and industry. In the 1960s computers were large, complicated machines that required skilled technicians to program them and keep them running. Computers of the day could easily fill a room with consoles and racks of tape-drive units. Despite their size, early computers had limited memory and were slow when it came to processing information. To remedy this, software designers created shortcuts in their programs to help speed up the computers and conserve memory. One of these shortcuts was that programs would refer to years by only their last two digits: *1968* became *68*, *1970* became *70*, and so on. The idea worked well, and through the years, as computers became smaller, faster, and more essential to business, the two-digit year notation remained the accepted standard. No one gave it a second thought.

No one, that is, until the year 2000 approached. By the 1990s some programmers began to suspect that the two-digit year notation might cause a problem in the switch over to the new millennium. What would happen if computers thought the new year—which would be designated as *00*—was actually *1900* and not *2000*? This was a computer bug that could have disastrous consequences. By the late twentieth century, computers were everywhere: they guided airplanes safely through the skies, recorded millions of retail purchases and banking transactions every day, helped keep hospital patients alive, and even controlled the elevators in

Revelers celebrate the arrival of the new millennium in New York City's Times Square. A catastrophic computer malfunction predicted to usher in the first decade of the 2000s never materialized but, sadly, the decade experienced many truly catastrophic events.

big city skyscrapers. From the largest industrial plant to the smallest digital watch, computers virtually ran the world. If the bug caused computers to shut down at midnight on December 31, 1999, as some computer experts feared, the world could descend into chaos.

People began calling it the Millennium Bug or Y2K (Year 2000) Bug, and the news media pounced on the story. One ABC news report called it "a tiny glitch a lot of people say could literally blow the lights out on civilization."[1] Soon the bug became a full-blown Y2K crisis in the press. But beyond all the hype and hullabaloo, programmers were working tirelessly to make sure their computers would handle the changeover without a problem. By the last day of 1999, the United States had spent more than $100 billion in an effort to fix the Y2K Bug. But as midnight approached, no one really knew if the efforts would be successful.

When the clock finally struck 12:00, nothing happened. While revelers celebrated the turn of the new century, the world's computers continued to function normally. There were a few isolated problems, but most were minor and easily corrected. When weary partygoers finally went to bed, they could take comfort in the knowledge that all was well in the world. The Y2K crisis was the catastrophe that never happened.

A Dangerous World

The rest of the decade would not pass as peacefully as this. Catastrophes of various types—from terrorist acts to natural disasters, from pandemics to structural failures—would bring pain and devastation to human communities across the globe. The world had dodged a bullet when the Y2K Bug turned out to be little more than a fleeting nuisance; however, many more catastrophic "bullets" were waiting to strike.

Chapter ONE

Our Restless Earth

Solid and seemingly unchanging, the surface of the earth is constant in everyday life. But beneath this firm exterior lies a turbulent interior. Only when this interior breaks through in the form of earthquakes and volcanoes does the hidden power of the earth reveal itself.

The earth is composed of several layers, from the outer crust to the dense iron core at the center. The crust and the layer just below it, the upper mantle, are made up of huge rock slabs called tectonic plates. These plates are constantly moving at a rate of about 1 to 6 inches (2.5 to 15 cm) per year. Most of the time, the plates slide smoothly against each other at their boundaries. Yet sometimes two plates get stuck and massive forces begin to build up. When the plates can no longer resist these forces, a sudden release of energy causes shock waves to ripple through the earth's surface: an earthquake is born.

More than a million earthquakes occur throughout the world each year. The strength of an earthquake is measured either by the Richter scale or the newer moment magnitude scale. An earthquake of magnitude 2.0 would not be felt by most people. At magnitude 5.0, some structural damage to buildings will occur. An earthquake of magnitude 9.0 or higher would cause destruction and loss of life on a massive scale.

Many earthquakes take place in remote areas of the world, causing little damage. Others occur beneath the world's oceans, creating a huge series of waves called a tsunami. In 2004 one such powerful tsunami proved devastating for nations on the rim of the Indian Ocean.

Tsunami: Eruption Under the Sea

December 26, 2004, was a beautiful Sunday on the Indonesian island of Sumatra. Vacationers filled the seaside hotels, and children played on sparkling beaches. Meanwhile, local fishermen launched their small boats hoping for a good day's catch. But 150 miles (241 km) from this peaceful scene, the earth was in turmoil. For thousands of years two tectonic plates, the India plate and the Burma plate, had been sliding against each other as they drifted some 19 miles (31 km) beneath the Indian Ocean. Throughout this time stress was building up, forcing the Burma plate to bend beneath the India plate. At 7:58 a.m. the strain finally became too great and the Burma plate snapped. It burst upward along a line some 750 miles (1,207 km) wide, the third most powerful earthquake in history. Radiating from the epicenter of the 9.2 magnitude quake was a huge surge of water—a tsunami.

In the deep ocean where the quake occurred, the waves were small, no more than a foot (30 cm) tall. But tsunamis build up enormous energy and height once they reach shallow coastal waters. This one was heading straight toward the island of Sumatra at a speed of 500 miles per hour (805 km/h).

A Calm Before the Storm

For those enjoying their day at the beach, the approaching tsunami gave little warning. One strange phenomenon might have saved people had they only known what it meant. Shortly before the tsunami struck the coast of Sumatra, the ocean began receding from the shoreline. This was the trough, or low point, of the approaching wave, and many people were unwittingly lured into danger as they walked the beaches, looking at the exposed seabed and the many fish stranded there. For a fisherman named Bustami, the first sign of danger was the sound of the approaching wave. "I heard this strange, thunderous sound from somewhere," he later recalled. "I thought it was the sound of bombs."[2]

Minutes later the crest of the tsunami smashed into the coast of Sumatra. A wall of water 40 feet (12 m) high roared over the beaches, sweeping away everything in its path. Banda Aceh, on the northernmost tip of Sumatra, was the first city to feel the full impact of the tsunami. Isnie Rizal barely escaped the raging water. "I turned around to see the water coming into the city from two directions," he said. "The waves looked empty but on top they were carrying everything from cars to the roofs of houses. I ran."[3] The deadly wave smashed through the city and traveled 2 miles (3.2 km) inland, destroying cars, trains, and buildings and instantly killing tens of thousands of people. Trying to outrun the deadly wave was futile. People were thrown like rag dolls against trees and buildings. Others were simply engulfed by the huge wave, never to be seen again. Among those carried away by the tsunami was eight-year-old Meri Yuranda. As the wave approached, Yuranda's father put her and her sister on the roof of their house for safety. But the wave was too strong and the girls disappeared.

"Doomsday"

In the span of a few minutes, Banda Aceh was transformed from a lively city of more than two hundred thousand to a rubble-strewn wasteland. Fisherman Bustami put it succinctly: "It felt like doomsday."[4] Antonia Paradela, on vacation near Banda Aceh, got a firsthand view of the ruins:

Tsunami survivors rummage through seemingly endless piles of debris in Banda Aceh in Indonesia on December 31, 2004, just days after a powerful earthquake set off a massive tsunami that killed more than 230,000 people in countries lining the Indian Ocean.

The scene there was one of total and absolute devastation. As we walked along a river we saw corpses floating. The fishermens' houses were totally leveled. Everywhere there were more and more corpses. . . . We walked for an hour witnessing big fishing ships that were thrown over buildings, and more and more bodies that lined the streets.[5]

In the quiet after the tsunami passed, those who escaped the deadly wave began searching the rubble for missing loved ones. This grim task did not always end happily. Isnie Rizal survived but lost his mother and three-year-old son. "I don't know why this happened," he said. "There's no one in this city that hasn't lost a close relative. . . . Nothing will ever

Tsunami Early Warning

In 1946 an earthquake off the Aleutian Islands in Alaska produced a tsunami that killed 165 people in Alaska and Hawaii. As a result of this tragedy, the Pacific Tsunami Warning Center (PTWC) was established to provide warnings to member nations of impending tsunamis. The center uses sophisticated seafloor monitors that can detect signs of earthquake activity and relay information via satellite to PTWC headquarters in Hawaii, where warnings are issued.

In 2004, however, there was no system to warn citizens of the Indian Ocean tsunami that was heading toward Indonesia. According to Costas Synolakis of the *Wall Street Journal,*

The angry questions that hundreds of thousands of family members of victims are asking, especially in Sri Lanka and India, are "what happened?"—and "why did no one warn us before the tsunami hit?" The Pacific Tsunami Warning Center had issued a tsunami bulletin and had concluded that there was no danger for the Pacific nations in its jurisdiction. Why didn't it extend its warning to South and Southeast Asia? It is perhaps clear with hindsight that an Indian Ocean tsunami warning center should have been in place, or that the Indian Ocean nations should have requested coverage from the PTWC.

In 2006 the Indian Ocean Tsunami Warning System was established to provide early warning to Indian Ocean nations.

Costas Synolakis, "Why There Was No Warning," *Wall Street Journal,* December 29, 2004. http://online.wsj.com.

be the same."[6] Shortages of food, water, and proper sanitation threatened to increase the death toll.

While survivors in Banda Aceh were slowly recovering from the shock of the tsunami, the wave continued on its relentless path of destruction. Much of Thailand was spared due to its location east of Indonesia, where it was sheltered from the brunt of the tsunami. But the coastal resort city of Phuket was hit hard by the wave, with a death toll as high as ten thousand and massive damage to the local tourism and fishing industries.

About two hours after it struck Sumatra, the tsunami smashed into the island of Sri Lanka, where 1.5 million people lost their homes. The death toll reached over 30,000, including some 2,000 people who perished in a train when the wave struck. In India more than 10,000 died, and thousands more were missing or homeless. Seven hours after the earthquake, the tsunami struck the east African country of Somalia, more than 3,000 miles (4,828 km) from the epicenter. Coastal villages were swept away, some eight hundred buildings were destroyed, and hundreds lost their lives. The destruction of hundreds of boats took away the livelihoods of countless Somali fishermen.

Disaster and Relief

An estimated 230,000 to 310,000 people lost their lives in the Indian Ocean tsunami, making it the worst tsunami in history and the fourth most devastating natural disaster since 1900. Approximately one-third of the dead were children, leaving grief-stricken parents behind. Others were orphaned, left to fend for themselves or find shelter in makeshift refugee camps. Twelve nations were affected by the tsunami to some degree. More than 1.5 million people were without a home, losing their possessions and, in many cases, their livelihoods. If there is a bright side to this catastrophe, it is the international humanitarian efforts mobilized as a response to the tsunami. Within days disaster relief was under way as military helicopters from the United States, India, Malaysia, and other nations delivered food, water, and medicine to beleaguered areas. The World Food Programme, a United Nations (UN) organization, delivered 123 million tons (111.5 million t) of food to more than 2 million survivors within six months of the tsunami. Governments around the world pledged some $4 billion in aid to the ravaged nations.

Memories of the tsunami lingered for years. For a fifteen-year-old Sumatran girl named Wati, those memories were of being separated from her family by the tsunami at the age of eight. In December 2011 Wati finally decided to try to find her parents. A chance encounter in a café in Meulaboh, a town near Banda Aceh, led Wati to a house and to a new life. "When I saw my mother, I knew it was her. I just knew it,"[7] she said. After seven years, Wati was reunited with her parents and learned her real name: Meri Yuranda. In the aftermath of so much pain and sadness caused by the Indian Ocean tsunami, at least one story had a happy ending.

Earthquake: "Ten Seconds of Terror"

For decades India and Pakistan have clashed over control of Kashmir, a territory in the northwest part of southern Asia beneath the Himalayas. Each nation has jurisdiction over parts of Kashmir, and the border between those parts has seen fighting for decades.

Deep below the disputed political border lies a geographical border between two tectonic plates. At 8:50 a.m. on October 8, 2005, the plates violently shifted, unleashing a 7.6 magnitude earthquake about 12 miles (19 km) from the town of Muzaffarabad, Kashmir's regional capital. The quake shook the ground as far away as Kabul, Afghanistan, some 245 miles (394 km) away. Geologist Fuzail Siddiqui was in Lahore, Pakistan, 200 miles (322 km) from the epicenter, when the tremor struck. "I realized it was an earthquake and instinctively rushed downstairs and onto the road. The ground ebbed and swelled under their feet as neighbours stood terrified on the roadsides. We felt muffled thuds under our feet and a low but distinct growl was heard. . . . These ten seconds of terror felt like an eternity."[8]

It was the worst earthquake to hit Kashmir in seventy years, affecting an area of about 11,500 square miles (29,785 sq km). "We are hearing reports of up to 80 and 90 percent of the affected areas' buildings being destroyed," UN Disaster Assessment and Coordination team spokesman Andrew Macleod said at the time. "There is going to be a huge number of people in need of food, water, and shelter."[9]

Initial casualty reports indicated that twenty thousand people had been killed by the quake. But those numbers grew as the true magnitude of the catastrophe began to unfold. "The situation is very, very bad," reported Riffat Pasha of the North-West Frontier Province police. "There are bodies lying everywhere. Those who have survived are lying in the open without food, shelter or medicine. The situation has been made worse by the rain and hailstorm that followed the earthquake. There is no way we can reach out to them."[10]

A Lost Generation

The earthquake struck on a Saturday, which is a school day in Pakistan-administered Kashmir. Jawad Khan was sitting in his public school classroom when the earthquake hit. All around Jawad and the other students, the building trembled, then collapsed. Khan lay trapped for two hours under the rubble of the school until rescue came. Although he survived, his life was forever changed by the earthquake. Khan's legs were so damaged that a year after he

---

ShakeOut Earthquake Drills

On April 4, 2009, alarms announcing an earthquake sounded in schools throughout northern India. Students scrambled under their desks, waiting to be evacuated to safety. Once outside, teachers counted their students, looking for any missing or injured pupils. Fortunately, no students were harmed because this was not a real earthquake. It was the first annual Kangra earthquake anniversary school safety ShakeOut drill.

Established in cooperation with GeoHazards International and GeoHazards Society of India, the annual exercise commemorates a devastating 1905 earthquake that shook India's Kangra Valley, killing nearly 20,000 people and destroying 100,000 structures. By practicing what to do if an earthquake strikes, children will be less likely to panic and suffer serious injury or death. "If we are prepared, it gives you an automatic sense of calmness," says student Yangzom. "So practicing earthquake drills is extremely important as there will be less panic, fear and anxiety. Hence, lesser casualties when the real one strikes."

The idea of earthquake awareness is not limited to India, nor are the drills just for schools. ShakeOut drills are conducted in many communities where earthquakes are likely to occur. California, Alaska, Oregon, Washington, and other states have their own ShakeOut drills, as do Canada, Japan, New Zealand, and numerous other nations. In 2012, more than 12 million people took part in ShakeOut drills worldwide.

Quoted in GeoHazards International and GeoHazards Society, India, "The Tibetan School Shake-Out," April 4, 2009. www.geohaz.in/upload/files/Tibetan_School_Shake_Out_Report1.pdf.

was pulled from the rubble, they had to be amputated. A donated wheelchair allowed him to get around, but after years of rolling over rough terrain it began to fall apart, and his parents could not afford to buy a new one.

Ali Khan was five years old when the earthquake injured his legs. While he could get around on crutches, his school was so far away that he could not attend. His once-cherished dream of becoming an engineer was destroyed by the disaster in Kashmir. Seven years after the quake, he put his plight into perspective. "This is fate. I have to live with it, and I just help my father the best I can around our farm. This is all that is left for me now."[11]

Jawad Khan and Ali Khan (they are not related) are just two of an estimated twenty-three thousand children left disabled by the earthquake. As the days wore on, the toll on the youth of Kashmir became far worse: seventeen thousand children were killed in the earthquake. As General Shaukat Sultan, Pakistan's military spokesman, reported, "It is a whole generation that has been lost in the worst affected areas."[12]

Aftershock

The damage caused by an earthquake does not always end when the ground stops shaking. Often the ground continues to tremble in a series of aftershocks that may last for hours or days after the initial tremor. Two hours after the Kashmir earthquake, an aftershock measuring 6.2 rocked the region. Dozens of other aftershocks followed, some as large as magnitude 5.0, causing panic among survivors fearful of a new, massive shock. The earthquake and aftershocks created another dangerous situation: landslides. The people of Kashmir "live at the bottom of these very, very steep canyons, so that earthquake-triggered landslides are common,"[13] explains Brian Tucker, president of relief organization GeoHazards International. The 2005 earthquake produced thousands of landslides that devastated 3,000 square miles (7,770 sq km) of mostly rural parts of Kashmir. Farmers in these areas lost their barns and other farm buildings, their livestock, and, in many instances, their lives. One huge slide buried four villages under 104.6 million cubic yards (80 million m³) of rock and debris. In all, tens of thousands of people died as a result of landslides.

The landslides also wreaked havoc on the region's infrastructure. Huge boulders and other debris blocked roads and collapsed bridges, making it difficult for rescue workers to get to the victims. Survivors could not communicate with the world outside the devastated area due to downed telephone lines. Electricity and water supplies were also cut off, making the ordeal even worse for people who had lost everything.

The statistics of the 2005 Kashmir earthquake are staggering. Some 86,000 people were killed, with another 100,000 injured. Most buildings in the region were not constructed to withstand earthquakes. A total of some six hundred thousand structures, including homes, hospitals, businesses, and government buildings, were either destroyed or irreparably damaged, a toll in excess of $6 billion. All this was made worse by the weather. Immediately after the earthquake, storms made it difficult for helicopters to fly in much-needed food and medical supplies. More than 3 million people found themselves homeless as the bitter Himalayan winter approached.

Earthquakes occur every day, most of them so mild that they go virtually unnoticed. The earth, however, has an even more spectacular way of showing off its might. Volcanoes can lie dormant for hundreds of years. Yet when they erupt, they are awesome displays of nature's power that can be as beautiful as they are deadly.

Catastrophe in the Congo

Virunga National Park in the Democratic Republic of Congo is home to one of the world's most fascinating geological sites. Mount Nyiragongo is an active volcano 11,385 feet (3,470 m) high, with a crater measuring 1.3 miles (2 km) in diameter at its summit. Inside the crater lies the world's largest lava lake, a glowing pool of red-hot molten rock at a temperature of 2,190°F (1,199°C). Hardy tourists come from all over the world to view this spectacular sight, beginning their trek in the nearby city of Goma. But on January 17, 2002, Goma, with a population of about five hundred thousand, was in danger of being wiped off the map.

At 9:30 that morning Mount Nyiragongo erupted. It was not the classic image of a volcanic explosion, with roiling clouds of debris shooting high into the sky. Instead, it was a fissure eruption, where fractures opened up in the southern flank of the volcano, sending rivers of lava pouring through. Traveling at a speed of up to 40 miles per hour (64 km/h), the lava flow steadily advanced toward Goma. Everything in the lava flow's path—trees, buildings, and entire villages—was destroyed. In Goma, some three hundred thousand people fled to safety in the nearby rain forest or across the border to the neighboring nation of Rwanda. "This is going to be a human

A river of lava flows through Goma in the Democratic Republic of Congo in 2002. Lava from the nearby Mount Nyiragongo volcano set off explosions, destroyed homes, and forced tens of thousands of people to flee.

catastrophe," a UN official said of the refugees. "We have to find them shelter, put them up in camps. There's no electricity, no running water."[14]

"We're Suffocating"

When the lava reached Goma, it had grown into a stream 3,280 feet (1,000 m) wide and 6 feet (2 m) deep, cutting the town in two. About 15 million cubic yards (11.5 million m³) of lava covered the downtown area of the city. As the red-hot lava rolled over filling stations, gasoline explosions rocked the air. Half of Goma's airport lay under a thick blanket of lava. In addition to the lava, dangerous fumes from the volcano filled the air above the city. "The smell of sulfur is everywhere," said another UN official. "There are fissures opening up in the town which billow smoke. People are scared."[15] As he loaded a van with what possessions he could save, a young man named Steven remarked, "We're suffocating in this town, the smoke is killing us."[16]

Goma lies on the northern shore of Lake Kivu, one of the African Great Lakes. At a depth of 1,575 feet (480 m), it is the eighteenth deepest lake in the world. As the lava flow from Mount Nyiragongo spread through Goma and poured into Lake Kivu, thousands of people sought to escape by boat. Small craft of all kinds ferried refugees over water that the lava had heated nearly to the boiling point. While Lake Kivu became a lifeline for countless Goma residents, it also presented another kind of peril. Deep within the lake lie vast reserves of carbon dioxide and methane gas. Further rumblings from Mount Nyiragongo could cause these deadly gasses to be released into the atmosphere, smothering thousands of people. "The carbon dioxide . . . is dangerous in concentrations of just a few per cent," said a UN volcanologist. "That would suffocate all living creatures."[17] One such disaster occurred in Cameroon in 1986, causing seventeen hundred deaths. The refugees from Goma wondered if this new threat would add to their misery.

"A Dead Town"

Fortunately, Lake Kivu remained calm and no gas was released. The day after Mount Nyiragongo erupted, people who had escaped the lava flow began returning to Goma. They were greeted by the eerie silence of a city partly covered by hardened lava that rose 7 feet (2.1 m) high in some areas. Fires still burned throughout the city, and rubble from destroyed buildings made it difficult to get from one place to another.

Most of the refugees were eager to learn if their homes had been spared. "My rented house is OK," observed one resident upon returning to Goma. "But there is no power, no drinking water, no food and no trade. It is a dead town."[18] Many other refugees were not so lucky. With their homes destroyed, thousands were forced to live in makeshift refugee camps. Food and fresh drinking water were scarce. Some people took to drinking water from Lake Kivu, despite warnings from officials that it was not healthy.

In the aftermath of the Mount Nyiragongo eruption, life went on. New houses were built directly on top of the solidified lava, but thousands of people remained homeless. Thirty to 40 percent of Goma was destroyed by the eruption. Thousands of buildings were destroyed, and about 245 people lost their lives. Tremors from Mount Nyiragongo continue to shake Goma, reminding its citizens of the awesome power of the restless earth. Italian volcanologist Dario Tedesco has called Goma "the most dangerous city in the world."[19] Ignace Madingo, a district administrator, accepts his city's fate. "We know the mountain will erupt again. Lava will come. Our homes will burn. And after, we will build once more."[20]

Chapter TWO

Killer Weather

In the classic film *The Wizard of Oz*, a young girl and her dog (as well as her entire house) are swept up by a huge tornado and deposited in an enchanting land of Munchkins, witches, and a not-quite-wonderful wizard. The film is a fantasy, of course, but the early scene of the huge tornado is a frighteningly realistic depiction of the power that weather can unleash.

Meteorological disasters occur when winds, rain, temperatures, or other natural phenomena exceed their normal boundaries and cause damage to life or property. Nature creates not only gentle breezes but also the devastating whirlwinds of tornadoes and hurricanes. Warm summer afternoons can turn into deadly heat waves. Quiet streams and rivers, when swollen by excessive rainfall, can overrun their banks and cause catastrophic flooding.

The science of meteorology is able to predict approaching weather systems with great accuracy, thanks to modern technology and a better understanding of weather patterns. Yet despite scientific advancements, nature often remains unpredictable. A rainstorm that was forecast to last for a day might continue for many days, creating the possibility for flooding. A tropical storm might remain small, or it might grow into a full-blown hurricane. Although hurricanes usually progress along a path that can be predicted, they may abandon that track, moving away from—or toward—inhabited land.

The founders of the city of New Orleans were not thinking of hurricanes when they established the city. Their thoughts were of commerce, and its location on the Mississippi River and Lake Pontchartrain, which leads to the Gulf of Mexico, made New Orleans an ideal trading outpost. Unfortunately, it also made it a sitting duck for deadly hurricanes.

A Catastrophe Named Katrina

The storm that would become known as Katrina began more than 4,600 miles (7,403 km) from New Orleans as a tropical depression, a small storm that formed off the western coast of Africa. Hot desert air mixed with the seasonally warm waters of the Atlantic Ocean, surging upward and producing strong winds and clouds. The storm grew as it began its journey westward; the rotation of Earth set it slowly spinning in a counterclockwise direction.

The storm reached the Bahamas on Tuesday, August 23, 2005. Meteorologists at the National Weather Service named it Tropical Depression 12. Although the storm was moving slowly, it picked up energy from the warm Caribbean waters. By Thursday, August 25, winds inside Tropical Depression 12 reached 75 miles per hour (121 km/h). This officially made it a Category 1 hurricane, the lowest of five steps on the Saffir-Simpson scale used to grade hurricanes.

An Ominous Warning

At 5:00 p.m. the storm struck Florida bearing 80-mile-an-hour (129 km/h) winds and a new name: Hurricane Katrina. At the National Hurricane Center in Miami, director Max Mayfield knew that Katrina could grow dangerously. "The fact that we had a major hurricane forecast over or near New Orleans is reason for great concern."[21] On Saturday, August 27, Mayfield placed a call to New Orleans mayor Ray Nagin, advising him to evacuate the city.

By Sunday, August 28, Katrina had grown to a Category 5 hurricane—the strongest on the Saffir-Simpson scale—with 160-mile-per-hour (257 km/h) winds. At 10:11 a.m. the National Weather Service issued an urgent warning:

> Devastating damage expected . . . most of the area will be uninhabitable for weeks . . . perhaps longer. At least one half of well constructed homes will have roof and wall failure. . . . All wood framed low rising apartment buildings will be destroyed. . . . Power outages will last for weeks . . . water shortages will make human suffering incredible by modern standards.[22]

Mayor Nagin knew that his city was in peril. About 80 percent of New Orleans lies 5 to 10 feet (1.5 to 3 m) below sea level. The city is surrounded by a system of levees that hold back the water from the Mississippi River on the south and Lake Pontchartrain on the north. The water driven ashore by a hurricane, called a storm surge, could overwhelm these levees and inundate the city. With Katrina bearing down, Nagin issued an order to evacuate New Orleans, the first such mandate in the city's history. "I wish I had better news, but we're facing the storm most of us have feared," Nagin said. "This is very serious. This is going to be an unprecedented event."[23]

Evacuating a city of nearly half a million residents was not an easy task. By noon the roads around New Orleans were jammed with people fleeing the city. But many residents, especially the poor, had no way to escape. "I know they're saying 'get out of town,' but I don't have any way to get out," lamented seventy-four-year-old Hattie Johns. "If you don't have no money, you can't go."[24]

Those without a means of transportation were instructed to seek shelter in the city's enclosed sports arena, the Louisiana Superdome. More than ten thousand people in the Superdome, as well as those who could not or would not leave their homes, spent an anxious night waiting for Katrina to arrive.

Landfall

If there was any good news for New Orleans on the morning of August 29, 2005, it was that Hurricane Katrina did not directly hit the city. The storm, now a Category 3 but still massive, made landfall at 6:10 a.m. near the Louisiana town of Buras, about 50 miles (80 km) east of New Orleans. Its sustained winds of 125 miles per hour (201 km/h) uprooted trees, toppled power lines, and damaged or destroyed nearly everything in its path. The hurricane stripped whole roofs off houses, damaged high-rise buildings, and hurled all manner of objects through the air, including appliances, light vehicles, and building debris.

Katrina punched two holes in the roof of the Superdome. Then the power went out, leaving the refugees inside without air conditioning. As more and more people sought refuge there, the population in the stadium climbed to nearly twenty-five thousand. Heat and the lack of food and water made conditions almost unbearable. Sanitation became a major problem as the dome's restrooms were overwhelmed.

Soon, what everyone feared the most began to happen. Reports of breached levees started coming in: first the Seventeenth Street Canal levee, then the levees at the Industrial Canal and the London Avenue Canal.

By the next day 80 percent of New Orleans lay under water that would soon become a toxic brew contaminated by raw sewage, chemicals, and other pollutants. In all, about one hundred thousand people remained in the ruined city. To escape the rising tide, many scrambled to their rooftops to await rescue. Some gathered in dark attics that provided no escape to the outside world. "We saw people sticking their hands outside through rafters," reported Mark Biello, a correspondent for CNN. "They are chopping through with axes on the rooftops to pull people that are literally just breathing the last air in their homes."[25] Many died in their attics before help could arrive. With the Superdome overcrowded, many people rescued from their homes were taken to the Ernest N. Morial Convention Center. Conditions there soon resembled those at the Superdome.

Water continued to pour into New Orleans from the breached levees. Helicopters began dropping sandbags and concrete blocks into the openings to stem the flow, but they were soon called away to help rescue people stranded on rooftops. Emergency workers used small boats to rescue survivors, sharing the flooded streets with rats, poisonous snakes, and dead bodies. Looters waded through waist-high water, breaking into stores and stealing items ranging from clothing, jewelry, and televisions to food. New Orleans police officers were ordered to suspend their life-and-death rescue missions to focus on the problem of looting.

The Aftermath

After flying over the stricken city, President George W. Bush declared, "We are dealing with one of the worst natural disasters in our nation's history."[26] And yet, one of the criticisms that arose in the aftermath of Hurricane Katrina centered on the response of federal officials to the crisis. The Bush administration seemed unprepared to deal with the catastrophe. An angry Mayor Nagin expressed his outrage in a radio interview. "This is ridiculous. . . . You mean to tell me that a place where you have probably thousands of people that have died and thousands more that are dying every day, that we can't figure out a way to authorize the resources that we need? Come

An Air Force Reserve team searches for survivors in New Orleans, where only the tops of houses are visible after levees built to protect the city burst open in 2005 during a raging Hurricane Katrina. The official death toll of the storm was 1,836; financial losses were estimated at $100 billion.

on, man."[27] Waiting for orders to evacuate refugees from the city, Air Force colonel Tim Parchick summed up his feelings of frustration: "Who's running things? Nobody, as far as I can tell."[28]

The agency responsible for "running things" was the Federal Emergency Management Agency (FEMA). Many people blamed FEMA and its director, Michael Brown, for delays in sending help to the

PERSPECTIVES

Human Activity Is Altering Earth's Weather

Super hurricanes, devastating floods, and record heat waves all seem to indicate that Earth's climate is changing—and not for the better. Global warming, hastened by human activity, is often singled out as the major cause of increasingly violent and deadly weather. A study by the Georgia Institute of Technology and the National Center for Atmospheric Research found that the occurrence of Category 4 and 5 hurricanes increased from 20 percent in 1970 to 35 percent in 2005. A study published in the journal *Nature* showed that as ocean temperatures rise, hurricanes become stronger.

Al Gore Jr., the former US vice president and an environmental activist, explains the predicament:

> Here is what scientists have found is happening to our climate: manmade global-warming pollution traps heat from the sun and increases atmospheric temperatures. These pollutants—especially carbon dioxide—have been increasing rapidly with the growth in the burning of coal, oil, natural gas and forests, and temperatures have increased over the same period. Almost all of the ice-covered regions of the Earth are melting—and seas are rising. Hurricanes are predicted to grow stronger and more destructive, though their number is expected to decrease. Droughts are getting longer and deeper in many mid-continent regions, even as the severity of flooding increases.

Al Gore Jr., "We Can't Wish Away Climate Change," *New York Times*, February 27, 2010. www.nytimes.com.

ravaged city. Brown appeared unaware of details of the disaster, such as the fact that the convention center had been opened to refugees. On September 12, about two weeks after the hurricane had made landfall, Brown became one more casualty of Hurricane Katrina: he resigned as the head of FEMA.

Hurricane Katrina left America's Gulf Coast decimated. Total monetary losses were estimated at $100 billion, more than any other catastrophe in American history. The official death toll is 1,836, but some estimates range up to 3,500; the real tally may never be known. Some

275,000 homes were damaged or destroyed. Nearly 80 percent of New Orleans residents left the city to seek safety. Some would eventually return, but the city's population would remain smaller than before Katrina. Finally, a little more than a month after Katrina had made landfall, New Orleans had dried out. Its citizens slowly returned to clean up debris and try to make a life once more.

PERSPECTIVES

Human Activity Is Not to Blame for Changing Weather Patterns

In the aftermath of Hurricane Katrina, many people cited the devastating storm as proof that global warming was adversely affecting Earth's weather and blamed human activity for those changes. Opponents of this view say that global warming is a recurring natural phenomenon that is not affected by human civilization. One aspect of the debate that is often targeted is the view that warmer ocean temperatures increase hurricane activity. While it is true that hurricanes are becoming more destructive, anti–global warming advocates say that this is a natural cycle of events that has been going on for millennia.

Max Mayfield, one of the foremost experts on climate and hurricanes, reported on these topics to the US Senate in the wake of Hurricane Katrina:

> The 1940's through the 1960's experienced an above average number of major hurricanes, while the 1970's into the mid-1990's averaged fewer hurricanes. The current period of heightened activity could last another 10-20 years. The increased activity since 1995 is due to natural fluctuations/cycles of hurricane activity, driven by the Atlantic Ocean itself along with the atmosphere above it and not enhanced substantially by global warming. The natural cycles are quite large with on average 3–4 major hurricanes a year in active periods and only about 1–2 major hurricanes annually during quiet periods, with each period lasting 25–40 years.

Max Mayfield, "Oversight Hearing on the Lifesaving Role of Accurate Hurricane Prediction," US Senate Committee on Commerce, Science, and Transportation, Subcommittee on Disaster Prevention and Prediction, September 20, 2005. www.legislative.noaa.gov/Testimony/mayfieldfinal092005.pdf.

Deadly Heat

With their howling winds and torrential rains, hurricanes are dramatic examples of nature's destructive fury. But not all catastrophes are so outwardly intense. Heat waves are not usually thought of as lethal, yet they are one of the most dangerous of all weather phenomena. According to the Earth Policy Institute, heat waves "claim more lives each year than floods, tornadoes and hurricanes combined. Heat waves are a silent killer, mostly affecting the elderly, the very young, or the chronically ill."[29] In August 2003 a withering heat wave quietly and relentlessly descended on Europe. The consequences were thousands of people dead, crops ruined, wildfires raging, and an investigation of one nation's health care system.

The western European climate is relatively moderate, with temperatures that seldom exhibit wide swings from hot to cold. For example, the average high temperatures in London range from 45°F (7°C) in January to 72°F (22°C) in July. But in July 2003 temperatures all over Europe began slowly climbing, reaching a record 118°F (48°C) in Portugal. Other western European nations experienced record high temperatures as well. One cause of this heat wave was the formation of an anticyclone, an area of high atmospheric pressure. Unlike a cyclone, which is a depression that moves and can create hurricanes, an anticyclone stays in one location for a long time. The anticyclone lingered over western Europe, producing clear days with little or no rainfall. An additional source may have been the warm water current known as El Niño, which had been especially active the previous winter.

Europe Swelters

Most Europeans were unprepared for the soaring temperatures. Living in such a relatively mild climate, they had no experience with blistering heat. Few homes, offices, and factories were air conditioned. To cope with the heat wave, people took cool baths or showers, drank large quantities of water or other cold beverages, and tried to stay indoors at midday, when the temperatures were the highest. Sales of air conditioners soared, and municipal power grids strained to keep up with the demand for electricity to run the units. Some people, desperate for relief, turned outdoor fountains into temporary wading pools. For those who had to work outdoors, the situation was all but unbearable. Stefano Colvolino's job as a traffic policeman in Rome kept him outside in the sweltering heat. "I haven't seen heat like this in 70 years," he said. "I'm out on the streets four hours a day. They're the four worst hours of the day."[30] In fact, all of Europe had not seen such high temperatures in over 450 years. In Spain the thermometer soared to 113°F (45°C), and Germany experienced a record 105°F (41°C). In July Italy hit a high of 115°F (46°C), and on August 10 the United Kingdom reached an all-time record temperature of 101°F (38°C). In mountainous Switzerland the heat wave caused unprecedented melting in the Alpine glaciers, causing numerous rock falls and landslides.

The heat also took a toll on the European economy. Rails buckled by the heat delayed trains carrying products to market. Crops were devastated due to the drought that accompanied the high temperatures. France alone lost 20 percent of its wheat output. But even worse than the loss of business was the human suffering and death toll from the effects of the heat wave.

A Tragic Toll

Ninety-two-year-old Paule de Noinville lived through the 2003 European heat wave. Although Sainte-Agnès, the retirement home where she resided, had no air conditioning, it did have one vital resource: caring people. The doctors and nurses at Sainte-Agnès provided the residents with cool drinks, wet towels, and ice packs. "We in this home are just lucky we had excellent people caring for us," she recalled. "They knew exactly what to do to make sure [we] came through fine. Not everyone was so lucky."[31]

The elderly suffered the most in the heat wave, especially in France, where more than fourteen thousand people died. The majority of French hospitals and nursing homes were not equipped to handle the stifling temperatures. Many frail elderly people who did not need constant care in a health facility lived at home, without family or friends. After weeks of unrelenting heat, they died alone in their apartments.

As the number of deaths rose, many blamed the French government for an inadequate response to the crisis. Hospitals were understaffed, and many physicians were away on their traditional August vacations when the heat wave struck. "The weakest are dropping like flies," criticized French physician Patrick Pelloux. "They [government officials] dare to say these deaths are natural. I absolutely do not agree."[32] Another doctor lamented, "We were not at all prepared—the hospital system is failing."[33] French president Jacques Chirac, who was vacationing in Canada during the crisis, received much of the criticism. "Everything will be done to correct the insufficiencies that we noted in our health system," Chirac said in a televised address. "Many fragile people died alone in their homes. To avoid these tragedies in the future, our prevention, surveillance and alert system will be reviewed so as to ensure greater effectiveness."[34]

After the heat finally began to subside in mid-August, European governments made plans for coping with future heat waves. Public cooling showers, temporary beaches, and opening air-conditioned buildings to provide relief for affected citizens were among the proposals. But future plans could not erase the consequences of the heat wave: the European agricultural and forest industry incurred $15 billion in damages, stocks of fish were depleted in warming rivers, and almost 1.6 million acres (647,497 ha) of forest land were destroyed by wildfires. But the human toll was the most tragic consequence. With at least thirty-five thousand deaths, the 2003 European heat wave lived up to its description as a silent killer.

Tornado Alley

The violent winds of a single tornado can tear roofs off houses and toss cars around like toys. When two or three tornadoes strike, the effect on a community can be devastating. Over a span of twelve days in the spring of 2003, more than four hundred tornadoes ripped through the central United States, causing massive destruction on a scale seldom seen, even in a region nicknamed "Tornado Alley."

There is no official description of the exact location of Tornado Alley. It is usually described as an area encompassing parts of Texas, Oklahoma, Colorado, Kansas, Nebraska, and Iowa. Many experts also include Illinois, Missouri, Arkansas, and other states as well. It is within this region that 90 percent of all tornadoes in the United States occur. Tornadoes form in severe thunderstorms, when cold, dry arctic air meets warm, moist tropical air. These conditions are common in Tornado Alley in the spring, creating a fertile breeding ground for tornadoes. In an average year about one thousand twisters touch down across the United States. In 2003 Tornado Alley recorded nearly half that number in less than two weeks.

The First Twisters

The convergence of an area of low pressure over the western United States and warm air from the Gulf of Mexico created a boundary between the two air masses. Severe thunderstorms can form along this boundary, which meteorologists call a dry line. A strong upper-level airflow can cause the winds in these storms to rotate; from this spinning air mass tornadoes are born. By the end of April 2003 conditions were ideal for the creation of tornadoes in the Midwest.

On April 30 about twenty tornadoes were spotted in Colorado, Iowa, Illinois, Missouri, and Kansas. These twisters were small, almost all measuring F0 on the Fujita scale, which rates the intensity of tornadoes. (F0 is the weakest; F5 is the most destructive.) Although some minor damage was reported, most of the tornadoes touched down harmlessly in open fields. Over the next several days more twisters arrived in Tornado Alley. Thirty tornadoes hit the ground, some with Fujita numbers of F1 and F2. A few trees and power lines were downed, and several vehicles and farm buildings sustained damage. So far, the tornado outbreak was rather mild with little destruction reported. All that would change on May 4, 2003.

The Worst Week

The atmospheric conditions for the creation of tornadoes converged that Sunday; a total of eighty-six twisters roared through parts of Missouri, Kansas, Arkansas, and Tennessee. Missouri suffered the most loss of life, with eighteen deaths attributed to the tornado. At 6:40 p.m. on May 4, tornado sirens wailed in Pierce City, Missouri, a town of about fourteen hundred. Twenty minutes later an F3 tornado slammed into the town, killing five and damaging or destroying most of the town's buildings. The entire historic business district was destroyed. Mike Allen watched the storm approach from his apartment doorway. "I saw like a black wall, I couldn't see the edges of it. It was eating those buildings. It was just ripping them apart and all the pieces up in the air like smoke."[35]

Tornadoes continued to roll through Tornado Alley, leaving a trail of death and destruction. On May 8 Oklahoma City was lashed by a

Dozens of violently swirling tornadoes, similar to the one pictured here in Minnesota in 2010, swept through the US region known as Tornado Alley in 2003. The tornadoes brought death and destruction to several states.

tornado that ranged in intensity from F2 to F4. Striking at rush hour, the storm tossed cars and created massive jams on interstate highways. A nearby General Motors plant was damaged, as well as hundreds of homes damaged or destroyed. More than twenty thousand residents lost electrical power. Over the next several days tornadoes ranging from F0 to F3 pummeled the state, leading President George W. Bush to declare the entire state of Oklahoma a disaster area.

By the end of the worst week, forty-four people had lost their lives and an initial estimate of damages topped $100 million. In all, more than four hundred tornadoes had moved through twenty-five states, the most ever recorded in a single outbreak. George Cullen, a meteorologist for CBS News, described it as "probably the most violent weather I've seen in the last 25 years, at least for an entire week."[36] Giving a speech in Little Rock, Arkansas, President Bush observed, "Nature is awfully tough at times, and the best thing we can do right now is pray for those who have suffered."[37] Among them was Gene Wilson, whose business sustained massive damage. "It's just devastating," he said. "My building and everything I've worked for 30 years is down on the ground."[38]

Wind, rain, heat all help to create the beauty of a flower or a refreshing breeze on a summer day. But when nature unleashes its fury, devastating destruction can turn nature into humanity's worst enemy.

Chapter THREE

Deadly Diseases

Everyone gets sick—it is a natural part of life. Most of the time the illnesses suffered by humans are not life threatening, as with the typical cold or flu. But sometimes an illness can grow to be so deadly and so widespread that it becomes a pandemic: an extensive outbreak of infectious disease that can afflict millions of people.

In 1918, as World War I was slowly grinding to a conclusion, a new disease appeared. Called the Spanish flu, it killed more people than all of the fighting in the war. The Spanish flu first spread through the ranks of soldiers at the battlefront. Before long a second, more deadly wave appeared and quickly spread around the globe, infecting some 500 million people. Most historians believe the Spanish flu killed 40 to 50 million people, although some estimates go as high as 100 million.

During the early twentieth century health care was relatively primitive compared to modern-day medical science. Diseases such as influenza are no longer life threatening for most people. But what if a new virus suddenly appears? A world population of over 7 billion people and the ease of international travel by air have created an ideal system for spreading new diseases around the globe with frightening swiftness. In 2003 another new disease made its appearance. It would become the first pandemic of the twenty-first century.

A Deadly Pneumonia

Carlo Urbani was the kind of physician who studied disease by going where the patients were rather than spending his time in a stuffy laboratory. That philosophy took Urbani to third-world countries working with desperately ill patients. "If I can't work in such situations," he once remarked, "what am I here for? Answering e-mails, going to cocktail parties and pushing paper?"[39] In February 2003 Urbani was working for the World Health Organization (WHO) in Hanoi, Vietnam. When he received a call one morning about an unusual case of the flu, he rushed to the hospital to see the patient.

At the hospital, Urbani thought the man might have something more serious than the flu. A recent outbreak of a mysterious pneumonia-like illness had been reported in China, and Urbani thought the symptoms of this case were similar. Could the disease have spread from China to Vietnam? Urbani soon had his answer as more people came down with respiratory symptoms. The disease was highly contagious, putting hospital personnel at great risk. Of the initial group of patients, more than half were health care workers. Panic began to set in. "I have a hospital full of crying nurses," Urbani told another doctor. "People are running and screaming and totally scared. We don't know what it is, but it's not the flu."[40]

A Global Threat

Reports of the new disease soon began coming in from Thailand, Singapore, Indonesia, the Philippines, and Hong Kong. The symptoms mimicked the flu: high fever, headache, muscle aches, and a cough or difficulty breathing. But antiviral medicines usually prescribed for the flu had no effect on the new disease. By March 11, 2003, more than 1,000 people had been infected worldwide, and more than 120 had died. Urbani was alarmed by the rapid spread of the disease, and he urged WHO to release a public warning. On March 15, the organization issued a global alert:

> During the past week, WHO has received reports of more than 150 new suspected cases of Severe Acute Respiratory Syndrome (SARS), an atypical pneumonia for which cause has not yet been determined. . . . "This syndrome, SARS, is now a worldwide health threat," said Dr. Gro Harlem Brundtland, Director General of the World Health Organization. "The world needs to work together to find its cause, cure the sick, and stop its spread."[41]

The swift spread of SARS was the greatest danger posed by the new virus. Just a few months after its discovery, the SARS virus had already been found in twenty-six nations. If scientists could not determine the source of the virus and how to halt its spread, the entire world could be affected.

Urbani was commended for being the first person to recognize the danger posed by SARS. His warning to WHO unquestionably saved countless lives. The one life he could not save, however, was his own. Due to his close work with infected patients, he contracted SARS and died on March 29, 2003.

The Crown Virus

The world had been alerted to a deadly new disease, but researchers still did not know how to treat it. Part of the problem was the fact that China had kept the world in the dark about the outbreak. Doctors knew that the first case of SARS appeared in November 2002 in Guangdong, China. There, in crowded markets selling livestock and poultry, a virus migrated from an animal to the initial victim, a forty-five-year-old man. The spiky exterior of the virus as seen under an electron microscope gives it the name coronavirus, after the Latin *corona*, meaning "crown." Coronaviruses multiply and mutate within the human body, affecting the respiratory tract and causing difficulty in breathing and coughing. When a person infected with SARS coughs or sneezes, the virus spreads, transmitting the disease to anyone nearby.

As SARS began to spread in China, the Chinese government minimized the severity of the outbreak. Information in the country was strictly controlled by the Communist Party, and any news that might reflect poorly on the nation—such as a scandal, a disaster, or a disease outbreak such as SARS—was downplayed by state news media.

The first Chinese news report of the new virus was published in January 2003 by a newspaper in the city of Heyuan. With typical disregard for the reality of the situation, the paper reported:

There is no need for people to panic. Regarding the rumor of ongoing epidemic in the city, Health Department officials announced at 1:30 a.m. this morning, "there is no epidemic in Heyuan." The official pointed out that people don't need to panic and there is no need to buy preventive drugs.[42]

SARS and the Economy

Despite this attempt to calm the citizens, people were indeed beginning to panic. On the streets of Beijing, in Hong Kong, and in countless other locales, people wore surgical masks as they went to work or school. Fear of SARS was spreading almost as fast as the disease itself, and it was

A deadly outbreak of SARS in 2003 prompted fears of widespread contagion. Health experts searching for the origin of the outbreak identified a crowded livestock and poultry market in China as the likely source of the disease. Here, a vendor sorts through chickens at a poultry market in China.

crippling the economies of nations hit by the virus. The Asian tourism industry felt the impact of SARS the most. Airlines saw a 70 percent drop in flights to Asia; the hotel and restaurant industries experienced a catastrophic decline in business. The cost to the economies of Asian nations was estimated at $60 billion.

Even in the United States, where few SARS cases were recorded, the stock market slumped amid worries of further economic decline caused by the disease. In Canada, where some 250 cases emerged, fear of SARS spreading further was costing the country an estimated $30 million per day. People worried that the global economy might collapse if SARS was not stopped.

An Emerging Global Epidemic

The new decade of the 2000s brought with it a new global health epidemic that could affect 370 million people worldwide by 2030. Diabetes has been called the silent killer because it displays few symptoms as it damages the body. Type 2 (sometimes called adult onset) diabetes is due in large part to obesity and lack of exercise. It is estimated that 200 million people around the world suffer from diabetes.

Thomas Novotny, a professor of epidemiology at San Diego State University, discusses the global implications of diabetes:

> Epidemiologists have been tracking this for some time and realized that there's a lot of transitions that are in place. One is that people are growing older and so it makes sense that diseases such as diabetes that affect older populations are going to be more prevalent. . . . There have been a number of influences that have been recognized in terms of globalization, things like changes in the way we work, our physical output, in terms of calories used. Our diets have become globalized so that we've changed from a lot of complex carbohydrates to more fatty and sugar-laden foods. And so we've seen these trends in terms of behavior, urbanization, globalization, and so it's not surprising that a disease such as diabetes has become more prominent, and I think we've been seeing this come for at least a decade.

Quoted in KPBS Radio, "Diabetes: Global Health Epidemic of the 21st Century," April 27, 2010. *These Days*. www .kpbs.org.

Fortunately, things were changing in China. In April a doctor named Jiang Yanyong leaked to the American press the fact that there were far more cases of SARS in China than the government had admitted. China soon went from denying that SARS existed to declaring an all-out war on the disease. Throughout China, schools, cafés, and libraries were closed, and mass gatherings were banned. About 30,000 people were quarantined in Beijing and another 10,000 in Nanjing. Online learning was instituted for the nearly 2 million Chinese children whose schools were shuttered.

An End in Sight

As these containment measures began to take effect in China, the number of SARS cases started declining. In affected countries around the world, similar measures were having a positive effect. Nations were declared SARS-free as health officials reported no new cases. By June Hong Kong and most of China were declared free of the disease; in July Canada and Taiwan joined the growing number of SARS-free nations. The last case of SARS in the 2003 outbreak was isolated on April 22. After a minor outbreak of four people infected in January 2004, no further cases have been reported outside of a laboratory environment.

SARS infected a total of 8,098 people worldwide, causing 774 deaths and massive economic damage. SARS has not been seen since, and some people think that it has vanished for good. "We'd be lucky to believe that," commented SARS researcher Julie Hall, "and that would be very nice, but there is no research to support that."[43] The world's first outbreak of SARS had been contained, but the possibility of its return still exists.

Swine Flu

The tiny village of La Gloria lies about 250 miles (402 km) from the Mexican capital of Mexico City. Home to some three thousand residents, La Gloria is surrounded by mountains and pig farms, including one of the largest pig farms in the region. The stench from the farm drifts over the dusty town, but the residents of La Gloria have long since learned that they can do nothing but live with it.

Flu season in La Gloria usually comes and goes during the winter months. But when about 60 percent of the townspeople became ill in March 2009, Mexican officials began to take notice. Most of the afflicted residents of La Gloria were suffering from ordinary influenza. But in one patient, the flu was caused by a new kind of virus called H1N1. This virus often appears in pigs, which gives it the name swine flu. "In this case," reported Mexico's health secretary, José Angel Córdova, "there's a patient who turned out to be positive for the swine flu virus."[44] That patient was four-year-old Edgar Hernandez, the first documented case of the disease.

H1N1 influenza is different than the common flu experienced by most people. It is caused by a combining, called reassortment, of several different genes that can create a new virus inside the cells of pigs or other animals. This new virus may spread to humans, which can create a health problem. "Any time that there is a virus which changes," explains Gregory Hartl of WHO, "it means perhaps the immunities the human body has built up to dealing with influenza might not be adjusted well enough to dealing with this new virus."[45] The swine flu that struck Mexico was similar to the 1918 Spanish flu virus, but not as deadly. Hernandez eventually recovered from his illness. By that time, however, the swine flu had already spread beyond La Gloria.

The Danger Spreads

The number of cases of swine flu had been growing in Mexico since February 2009. Health Secretary Córdova said that Mexico had 56 confirmed deaths out of 2,059 confirmed cases. But those numbers were questioned; one scientific journal estimated that there may have been as many as 32,000 cases of swine flu in Mexico by April 23. Other cases were reported in Cuba, China, Finland, New Zealand, and Thailand. The Centers for Disease Control and Prevention (CDC) in Atlanta, Georgia, confirmed 40 cases affecting people in the United States. Authorities estimated that up to 40 percent of the US working population could ultimately get swine flu. In most instances, the flu was spread by travelers returning from Mexico. "It is clear that this is widespread," announced Anne Schuchat, director of the CDC's National Center for Immunization and Respiratory Diseases. "And that is why we have to let you know that we cannot contain the spread of this virus."[46] President Barack Obama declared a national emergency.

Mexico City subway commuters wear surgical masks as a precaution against swine flu in 2009. To help contain the epidemic, which spread from Mexico to countries as distant as Finland and New Zealand, the Mexican government temporarily closed schools, libraries, and other public places.

In Mexico City, where cases of swine flu were growing daily, the government urged citizens to stay indoors if they felt ill. People began avoiding large groups, where there might be carriers of the virus. Surgical masks became a common sight on the streets of the national capital. Handshakes and kisses, both a means of transmitting the virus, were frowned upon.

Schools, libraries, and museums were closed in order to eliminate crowds gathering in enclosed spaces where the flu might circulate.

The mood of the people ranged from worry and confusion to outright fear. "The people are scared," commented Roberto Ortiz, a physician in Mexico City. "A person gets some flu symptoms or a child gets a fever and they think it is this swine flu and rush to the hospital."[47] Government "cleaning brigades" began spraying disinfectants in subways, schools, and other public places in an effort to stop the spread of swine flu. Many Mexican citizens became angry at the government, say-

The World Health Organization

When a disease like SARS becomes a global threat, it takes a global organization to coordinate resources and provide leadership to combat the disease's spread. For more than sixty years WHO has been at the forefront of public health.

WHO was established by the United Nations in 1948 as a response to widespread disease and neglected health problems in the aftermath of World War II. Its history includes many highlights, including the eradication of smallpox, the reduction of deaths from tuberculosis, and the development of strategies to combat HIV/AIDS worldwide.

Margaret Chan, director general of WHO, noted the organization's efforts against HIV/AIDS:

> In less than a decade, the price of [AIDS] medicines dropped by 99%. WHO streamlined, simplified, and standardized treatment protocols, making it increasingly easy to get good treatment results in poor settings. Today, some 8 million people in low- and middle-income countries are receiving antiretroviral therapy for AIDS.
>
> In a just society, people should not die for unfair reasons, including an inability to pay for medicines. Making life-prolonging treatment available to millions of poor people was the right and moral thing to do. Fighting HIV/AIDS was never only about medicine and science. This was a social mission built on a respect for human rights and the dignity of every single life.

Margaret Chan, "Breaking the Cycle of Poverty, Misery, and Disease," World Health Organization, November 13, 2012. www.who.int.

ing that officials had waited too long in notifying the public about the H1N1 outbreak. Government health workers, overwhelmed by the increased number of hospital patients, demanded raises and better working conditions.

An End in Sight

The CDC had been working hard on the swine flu problem. On April 21 it activated its Emergency Operations Center in Atlanta to coordinate with the ongoing investigation. After analyzing samples from infected people, scientists discovered that the swine flu was resistant to two common antiviral drugs but was susceptible to two other drugs—oseltamivir and zanamivir. The US government purchased 50 million doses of the latter medicine in case mass distribution became necessary. The CDC also began developing a virus that could be used to create a new vaccine to combat H1N1. The CDC shared the results of its investigations with researchers in other countries so they could combat local outbreaks.

In a June 11, 2009, press conference, Margaret Chan, director general of WHO, announced that "on the basis of available evidence . . . the scientific criteria for an influenza pandemic have been met."[48] The pandemic was now official. Pharmaceutical companies began manufacturing antiviral vaccines to protect people from H1N1. The plan was to make enough doses for everyone in the United States, but it soon became clear that it would take longer than expected. By October there was only enough vaccine to protect 20 percent of the US population. Only certain people—health care workers, children, the elderly, and people who were already ill—would get the vaccine first. Eventually the vaccine supply increased, and by December 2009 some 100 million doses were available. Swine flu was finally on the wane, leaving over 12,220 deaths worldwide in its wake.

In Mexico, where it all started, schools and other public places had reopened. WHO praised measures taken by the Mexican government during the outbreak. The closing of public spaces and sharing of swine flu data with other countries helped give the world early warning of the pandemic. The cost to Mexico was estimated at $3.5 billion.

In the town square of La Gloria stands a bronze figure of a little boy holding a frog. It is a statue of Edgar Hernandez and is called by some *El*

Niño Cero, meaning "Little Boy Zero," the first to be identified as having swine flu. The statue depicts Hernandez as a smiling, happy child, for he survived the swine flu pandemic. Sadly, many others around the world were not so fortunate.

Cholera: A Preventable Disaster

On December 11, 2008, Robert Mugabe, president of the African nation of Zimbabwe, boldly declared that his country was free of the terrible disease known as cholera. "There is no cholera,"[49] Mugabe told the assembled media during a televised press conference. Yet one look around the impoverished nation told a very different story. Amid inadequate sanitation and the absence of clean drinking water, a deadly epidemic had taken hold of Zimbabwe. Sixteen thousand cases of cholera had been reported, resulting in more than 780 deaths. Medical care for the sick and dying was largely nonexistent. And compounding the tragedy was the fact that it all could have been prevented.

Cholera is caused by a bacterium called *Vibrio cholerae.* This microorganism infects a person who drinks water or eats food that has been contaminated by human feces. Once inside the body, *Vibrio cholerae* multiplies with astonishing speed in the small intestine. It attaches to the wall of the intestine and begins to produce a poison called cholera toxin. The toxin prevents the victim's body from absorbing water; in response, the body begins to flush massive quantities of liquid out of the system. The infected person may lose up to 5 gallons (19 l) of watery diarrhea a day. If this continues untreated, the person will die from dehydration, often within hours of the onset of symptoms.

A Simple Cure

Sometimes called the blue death—a reference to the color of a severely dehydrated person's skin—cholera affects some 3 to 5 million people worldwide each year. Fortunately, most of these cases can be successfully treated. While there are vaccines that can be used to control cholera, there is an easier and more economical way to attack the disease: rehydration. Simply put, rehydration means replacing the body's lost fluid. A solution of water, salt, and sugar given to a cholera patient orally can begin to reverse the effects of cholera almost immediately. In severe cases, the solution is administered intravenously. If given promptly when the symptoms of cholera appear, oral rehydration is effective in about 80 percent of cases.

Water, salt, and sugar can easily be purchased almost anywhere in the world. But in a desperately poor nation like Zimbabwe, such items are

Children in Zimbabwe collect stagnant water for use at home in 2008. Such water often contains sewage and human waste, which makes it an ideal breeding ground for cholera. A cholera outbreak killed thousands of people in Zimbabwe and neighboring South Africa in 2008 and 2009.

difficult to come by. Because of this, the death toll from the cholera epidemic of 2008 in Zimbabwe was much higher than the average. "We are seeing a very high fatality rate," said Caroline Hooper-Box, spokesperson for Oxfam, an international humanitarian organization. "At this point we are seeing between an eight and 10 percent fatality rate." According to WHO, the fatality rate in the rest of the world is about 2.5 percent. Added Hooper-Box, "Things are going to get quite a lot worse before they are going to get better."[50]

An Uncaring Government

Mugabe's election as prime minister (later becoming president) in 1980 changed the status of Zimbabwe, formerly known as Rhodesia, from a British colony to an independent nation. Zimbabwe had a strong economy and was one of the most agriculturally efficient countries in Africa. But beginning in 2000, the nation began to decline. Under Mugabe's disastrous economic policies, such vital government services as garbage collection and water treatment were abandoned. Hospitals went unstaffed because doctors and nurses were not being paid. Damaged water pipelines were neglected, leaving thousands without clean drinking water. Untreated human waste became a major problem. "Piles of waste litter the streets and clog intersections," reported Richard Sollom, a doctor with Physicians for Human Rights. "Steady streams of raw sewage flow through the refuse and merge with septic waste from broken pipes."[51] It was a situation ideal for cholera.

Within weeks of the outbreak in August 2008, cholera had spread to nearly every part of Zimbabwe and even to nearby South Africa. Thousands of cholera victims sought help where none could be found; many government hospitals had more corpses than living patients. Finally, on December 4, the Zimbabwean government declared a national emergency and sought help from international aid groups to fight the cholera outbreak. By that time more than nine thousand cases of cholera and 350 deaths were recorded. Many nations around the world donated funds to help fight the cholera epidemic. Organizations such as Doctors Without Borders and the International Committee of the Red Cross set up clinics to treat the ever-growing number of patients. At one clinic two hundred patients came for treatment in a seven-hour period. Yet even the clinics had trouble getting the items needed to treat the patients. Zimbabwe's unstable economy made it difficult to buy such basic supplies as rubber gloves. Clean water had to be brought in by the truckload while new wells were being dug.

Rehydration therapy helped slow down, and eventually end, the Zimbabwean cholera outbreak. By June 2009 about 128,000 cases had been recorded, with over fifty-six hundred fatalities. The outbreak eventually spread to South Africa, Zambia, Mozambique, and Botswana. What could have been an easily preventable outbreak of disease had turned into a deadly epidemic due to the apathetic government of a poor nation.

Chapter FOUR

Terrorism Strikes

In January 2010 Michael Hicks was looking forward to a trip to the Bahamas with his family. But before he could board his flight at Miami International Airport, Hicks was taken aside by officers of the Transportation Security Administration (TSA) and given a thorough pat-down search. The TSA, charged with keeping suspected terrorists off airplanes, maintains a no-fly list of people who are not allowed to board aircraft. Hicks's name is on this list. Yet he is hardly a threat to airline security: at the time of his Bahamas trip, Hicks was an eight-year-old Cub Scout. It was a different person with the same name on the no-fly list.

The TSA was established in the wake of the 9/11 terrorist attacks on the United States in 2001. Preventing terrorism is a big job, and mistakes like the searching of young Michael Hicks are bound to happen. But that is what the terrorists want: to disrupt the daily lives of innocent people by creating an environment of fear.

Terrorists have struck in every part of the world, in every century. In 1881 a band of terrorists killed Russian czar Alexander II. Explaining their actions, the terrorists wrote, "Alexander II, the tormentor of the people, has been put to death by us, Socialists. He was killed because he did not care for his people."[52] Taking credit for their attacks allows terrorists to instill fear in their enemies.

Terrorists have hijacked airliners and cruise ships, holding passengers hostage while presenting their demands to political leaders. Dying for their cause became a part of their plans, especially for terrorists with religious motivations. Suicide bombings were a common weapon in the jihad, or holy war, waged by radical Islamists. Between 2000 and 2004, 472 suicide attacks killed more than seven thousand people in Iraq, Afghanistan, Pakistan, and nineteen other countries. Almost three thousand of those died on a clear, sunny New York morning in September 2001.

A Symbol Attacked

New York City is America's hub of commerce. The New York Stock Exchange trades more than $153 billion worth of stock every day. In 1973 construction was completed on the World Trade Center in Lower Manhattan, a group of seven buildings centered around two identical 110-story skyscrapers known as the Twin Towers. While not very popular at first, the Twin Towers eventually became beloved symbols of New York's—and America's— economic vitality.

Just before 9:00 a.m. on September 11, 2001, viewers of the *Today* show heard anchor Katie Couric make a disturbing announcement. "We have a breaking news story. . . . A plane has just crashed into the World Trade Center here in New York City."[53] Live video showed a column of oily black smoke pouring from the North Tower. Similar announcements appeared on all television networks, which replaced their regular programming with nonstop news coverage. As the day wore on and reports poured in from the scene, what had happened at the World Trade Center became horribly clear.

Four Airplanes

At 8:46 a.m. American Airlines Flight 11 crashed into the World Trade Center's North Tower. Carrying eighty-seven passengers and crew, the aircraft struck the building between the ninety-third and ninety-ninth floors, completely disintegrating and leaving a gaping hole in the tower. Its twenty-four thousand gallons of jet fuel exploded on impact, causing a raging fire inside the tower. Seventeen minutes later, at 9:03 a.m., another plane, United Airlines Flight 175, with sixty on board, struck the South Tower between floors seventy-seven and eighty-five. A massive explosion sent a shower of debris and a cloud of fire and smoke out of the side of the building. With network cameras already focused on the World Trade Center, the impact of the second plane was watched by millions of viewers.

People wondered if this was a terrible accident or something more sinister. Before the crashes, some disturbing radio and inflight telephone messages had come from the two doomed aircraft. At 8:25 a.m. ground controllers in Boston heard someone say, "Nobody move. Everything will be okay. If you try to make any moves, you'll endanger yourself and the airplane. Just stay quiet."[54] It was apparently a message meant for the passengers of Flight 11, made by someone who mistakenly activated the plane's radio instead of its public address system.

Peter Hanson, a passenger on Flight 175, called his father, Lee. "I think they've taken over the cockpit," Hanson said. "An attendant has been stabbed—and someone else up front may have been killed. The plane is making strange moves."[55] Lee Hanson called the local police with the information, not knowing that the airplane his son was on would crash into the World Trade Center eleven minutes later.

Two other hijacked airplanes were a part of the 9/11 attacks. American Airlines Flight 77 was taken over by terrorists and crashed into the Pentagon, America's military headquarters in Arlington, Virginia. The impact killed everyone on board and many military and civilian personnel in the building. At 9:28 a.m. hijackers commandeered United Airlines Flight 93 after takeoff in New Jersey. On this flight, a group of courageous passengers tried to retake command of the plane. Their struggle prevented the hijackers from reaching their target, most likely the White House or the US Capitol. With their goal thwarted, the terrorists crashed the aircraft into an empty field in Shanksville, Pennsylvania, killing all on board.

The Towers Fall

At the World Trade Center, police cars, ambulances, and fire engines filled the rubble-strewn streets. First responders laden with rescue equipment headed into the towers as thousands of workers made their way to safety down the crowded stairwells. For those on the floors below the impact zones, evacuation was difficult but possible. For people trapped above the gaping holes in the towers, however, there was little hope of rescue. Fire and debris blocked the stairs leading down to safety. Observers on the ground watched in horror as people jumped to their deaths to escape the flames.

And then the unthinkable happened. At 9:59 a.m. the South Tower collapsed in a roiling cloud of smoke and debris. Eyewitness David Rohde described the scene: "First, a sharp crack and then what sounded, oddly, like a waterfall, thousands of panes of glass shattering as the north side of the tower buckled. Then a slow building rumble like rolling thunder that will not stop as the tower cascades toward the ground."[56]

Nearly thirty minutes later the same horrifying scene was reenacted as the North Tower fell in a pile of twisted steel and smoking wreckage. In one hour and forty-one minutes from the time of the impact of Flight 11, the symbol of America's financial strength was gone.

United Airlines Flight 175 crashes into the South Tower of New York City's World Trade Center as smoke pours from the North Tower on September 11, 2001. The 9/11 terrorist attacks on the United States killed about three thousand people and prompted the start of America's War on Terror.

The Patriot Act: A Necessary Safeguard

In October 2001, just weeks after the 9/11 terrorist attacks, the US Congress passed and President George W. Bush signed into law the USA Patriot Act. The law granted federal authorities greater freedom in gathering information about possible terrorist acts. Under the Patriot Act federal agencies have greater authority to monitor telephone calls and emails and seize information that they deem relevant to security investigations. It also strengthens immigration laws. California senator Dianne Feinstein said of the Patriot Act:

> Americans, to a great extent, have looked at Government, saying: Just leave me alone. Keep Government out of my life. At least that is the way it was before September 11. What I hear post–September 11 are people saying: What is my Government going to do to protect me?
>
> As we look back at that massive, terrible incident on September 11, we try to ascertain whether our Government had the tools necessary to ferret out the intelligence that could have, perhaps, avoided those events. The only answer all of us could come up with, after having briefing after briefing, is we did not have those tools. This bill aims to change that. This bill is a bill whose time has come. This bill is a necessary bill.

Dianne Feinstein, *The Congressional Record—Senate*, vol. 147, no.144, 107th Congress, October 25, 2001, p. S11033. www .justice.gov/archive/ll/subs/support/senschumer102501_3.pdf.

Devastation at Ground Zero

Authorities soon pieced together facts about the hijackers. They were nineteen radical Muslims who, backed by a terrorist organization known as al Qaeda, sought to destroy what was, in their eyes, a nation of infidels. Never had so many innocent lives been lost in a single incident. At the World Trade Center, 2,606 died, including 343 firefighters and 60 police officers. On the four hijacked airplanes, 246 passengers and crew lost their lives, and 125 people died at the Pentagon. In total, 2,996 people (including 19 hijackers) perished in the 9/11 attacks.

Fires burned for more than three months at ground zero, as the World Trade Center site had become known. More than 1.5 million tons (1.4 million t) of debris was eventually removed from the site in a cleanup operation costing an estimated $1.3 billion. Economically, New York lost $105 billion in the month after the attacks, and eighty-three thousand jobs had been wiped out. The New York Stock Exchange was closed for six days. When it reopened, it plummeted 685 points, the

PERSPECTIVES

The Patriot Act: Trampling Rights

From the moment it was signed into law on October 26, 2001, the USA Patriot Act has been the object of much criticism. Many people were afraid that the increased powers given to federal agencies by the act would be used to invade their privacy and take away their civil liberties.

Occasionally an incident would occur that seemed to support the critics' view. A California man named Barry Reingold got into a political debate at his gym, during which he criticized President George W. Bush. The next week FBI agents came knocking at his door.

The American Civil Liberties Union, an organization dedicated to defending individual liberties, had strong words about the Patriot Act:

> The Patriot Act vastly—and unconstitutionally—expanded the government's authority to pry into people's private lives with little or no evidence of wrongdoing. This overbroad authority unnecessarily and improperly infringes on Fourth Amendment protections against unreasonable searches and seizures and First Amendment protections of free speech and association. Worse, it authorizes the government to engage in this expanded domestic spying in secret, with few, if any, protections built in to ensure these powers are not abused, and little opportunity for Congress to review whether the authorities it granted the government actually made Americans any safer.

Michael German and Michelle Richardson, *Reclaiming Patriotism: A Call to Reconsider the Patriot Act.* New York: American Civil Liberties Union, 2009, p. 10.

largest one-day loss in its history up to that time. The total cost of the 9/11 terrorist attacks is estimated at over $5 trillion.

An Act of War

After 9/11, America was at war with terrorism. On the evening of September 11 President George W. Bush addressed the nation on television:

> Today, our fellow citizens, our way of life, our very freedom came under attack in a series of deliberate and deadly terrorist acts. . . . These acts of mass murder were intended to frighten our nation into chaos and retreat. But they have failed. Our country is strong. A great people has been moved to defend a great nation.[57]

The War on Terror focused on al Qaeda and its leader, Osama bin Laden. In October 2001 a coalition led by US military forces began air strikes against suspected al Qaeda strongholds in Afghanistan. In 2003 the war expanded to Iraq. More than six thousand military personnel, as well as twenty-three hundred civilian contractors and an untold number of Afghan and Iraqi civilians, lost their lives in the conflict. On May 2, 2011, US Navy SEALs invaded Osama bin Laden's private compound in Pakistan and killed the al Qaeda leader.

The 9/11 terrorist attacks shook the United States to its foundation. The term *terrorism* became a part of America's national vocabulary, and people of the Muslim faith were unjustly vilified, all because nineteen terrorists thought their actions would destroy the United States. Instead, they strengthened America's resolve and redefined the concept of the nation's adversaries. Instead of fighting against massive uniformed armies, America was forced to confront stealthy insurgents who target innocent civilians.

Terror in Paradise

The Indonesian island of Bali is a popular destination for travelers looking for an exotic locale with beautiful beaches and a rich indigenous culture. The Kuta district is Bali's busiest tourist attraction, with modern hotels, restaurants and nightclubs, and a bustling business district.

October 12, 2002, was a typical Saturday night, with crowds of tourists jamming the bars and clubs. At about 11:00 p.m. tourist Chris Beirne walked into Paddy's Pub, a popular night spot filled with 150 laughing, dancing customers. A few minutes later an explosion rocked the bar. "There was a flash," recalled Beirne, "a little bit yellow and white at the top. . . . Everybody was silhouetted, all the heads. I remember I was on the floor."[58] A few seconds later another blast detonated outside the Sari Club across the street from Paddy's. "All of a sudden there was a thud," a survivor later said. "The lights flickered and died, then it flickered, the noise started going again and this big orange cloud lit up the sky. . . . It was just a nightmare, people screaming, people on fire."[59] More powerful than the first bomb, the second explosion destroyed the Sari Club, damaged surrounding buildings, and blew a 3 foot (1 m) crater in the street. There were so many casualties, including a large number with extensive burns, that the local hospital could not handle the number of injured. Many victims had to be flown to Australia for treatment. In the span of a few seconds, paradise had turned into an inferno.

The Exploding Van

The Bali bombing of October 12, 2002, was the worst terrorist act in Indonesian history. Casualties totaled 202 killed and hundreds injured. Most of the victims were young tourists having a fun night out. Among the dead were 88 Australians, 38 Indonesians, 24 Britons, and 7 Americans. As officials surveyed the rubble of the two nightclubs, finding out who had done this—and why—was uppermost in their minds.

As Indonesian and Australian forensic investigators combed through the 47,000 square yard (39,298 sq m) blast site, they found debris from a Mitsubishi van, possibly the vehicle that carried the bomb. An identifying number on a piece of the destroyed van led to Amrozi bin Nurhasyim—a member of Jemaah Islamiyah, a radical Islamist group with ties to al Qaeda. Bin Nurhasyim had purchased the van and the explosives used in the Sari Club bombing. Eventually Bin Nurhasyim's accomplices were arrested, and the true story of a precisely timed terror attack emerged.

On the night of the bombings, two suicide bombers drove a white Mitsubishi L300 and parked it just outside the Sari Club. The rear of the van was filled with 2,425 pounds (1,100 kg) of explosives packed into plastic file cabinets. One of the men put on an explosives-laden vest and walked into Paddy's Pub. A few minutes later he detonated his vest, blowing himself up and killing dozens in the bar. As survivors of the blast fled Paddy's and ran into the street, the remaining bomber, still seated in the van, detonated his explosives. The blast ripped through the night, killing scores of people inside the Sari Club and on the street. A third bomb was detonated that night, a small explosive placed in front of the US consulate. The bomb did little damage.

Terrorism changes things. In Indonesia, a police antiterrorist unit was created to deal with the possibility of future attacks. A campaign to assure travelers that Bali is a safe vacation destination has brought tourism back to prebombing levels. The Sari Club is now gone, and a vacant lot stands in its place. Paddy's Pub was rebuilt at another location, and on its original site stands a memorial to those who died in the attack.

Attacks on Mass Transit

Public transportation systems are vital to large cities around the world. For that reason, the buses, trains, and subways that carry people to and from their jobs each day present an inviting target for terrorism. Hundreds of passengers packed into a confined space offer an attractive target for potential terror attacks. In the first decade of the 2000s, two European capitals became the focus of such terrorist plots.

Rush hour in Madrid is much like rush hour in any other big city. Commuters dash to get a space on buses and subway trains before they are filled to standing room only. March 11, 2004, was a typical workday in Spain's capital city. At about 7:40 a.m. a *cercanías*, or commuter train, entered the Atocha station in downtown Madrid. As it pulled to a stop, three explosions rocked the train, destroying three cars and sending acrid smoke through the station. A few seconds later four more bombs blasted a train that was just about to enter the station. The scene at the Atocha station was one of confusion and panic. "People started to scream and run, some bumping into each other," said one bystander. "I saw people with blood pouring from them, people on the ground."[60] But the terrorists were not finished. Within a few minutes bombs were detonated on two other trains at smaller stations. In all, ten bombs exploded in Madrid, the deadliest coordinated terror attack since 9/11.

Soft Targets

The Madrid bombs killed 191 people and injured more than 1,800. Like the 9/11 and Bali attacks, the bombings in Madrid were aimed at soft targets—average people in theaters, shopping malls, restaurants, and other vulnerable locations. And the carnage could have been much worse. Investigators found three more bombs at the Atocha station that were rigged with timers but failed to detonate. Had these bombs exploded as planned, hundreds of rescue workers would have been injured or killed and the entire Atocha station might have been destroyed.

Due to the precise nature of the Madrid bombings, officials suspected that they were the work of al Qaeda. Eventually twenty-eight men, most of them from Morocco, were put on trial for the bombings. Although al Qaeda was not directly involved, its influence on the bombers was clear. Twenty-one of the accused were found guilty, but seven, including the reputed mastermind of the attacks, were set free. Many Spaniards were angered over the acquittal. "It has destroyed my life," said Isabel Presa, whose son was killed in the bombing. "It has condemned me and my husband to a life sentence, and these people get off scot-free."[61]

Explosion in the Underground

The London Underground—the British name for the subway—was crowded on the morning of July 7, 2005. At the King's Cross station a young man wearing a backpack stepped onto a waiting train. His name was Germaine Lindsay, and inside his backpack was a homemade bomb powerful enough to destroy the train he had just boarded. Lindsay was not alone. Two other young men boarded other trains wearing deadly backpacks. Between 8:50 and 8:51 a.m. all three men detonated their bombs. The resulting explosions killed and injured scores of people and sent survivors scrambling for safety. Chris Lowry, who was on the train

Firefighters carry a body on a stretcher during efforts to rescue people injured when terrorist bombs exploded on crowded commuter trains in 2004 in Madrid, Spain. The attacks killed 191 people and injured more than 1,800.

at King's Cross, recalls that "a fat blast came from the front end. I actually think I fell out of my seat at first—all I could see was smoke."[62] Lowry made it to safety, but others were not so lucky; twenty-six people died on that train and hundreds were injured. Similar scenes played out in the other two bombed trains.

Almost an hour later, as rescue crews helped the injured and dying at the blast scenes, another bomb was detonated. Placed on one of London's famous red double-decker buses, the bomb tore the roof off the bus and killed thirteen people. Jasmine Gardner was about to board the bus when the bomb went off. "One minute the bus was there, the next minute it seemed to dissolve into millions of pieces. . . . I turned away because I couldn't face to look at it."[63] Fifty-six people lost their lives, and more than seven hundred were injured.

Homegrown Terrorists

When investigators examined surveillance video from cameras in the King's Cross station, they saw four men with large backpacks hug each other and then separate to board different trains. The men were later identified as Muslims of British citizenship: Germaine Lindsay and three other men with ties to Pakistan. The terrorists had assembled their bombs in a quiet neighborhood of London, never raising the suspicions of their neighbors. Their leader, Mohammad Sidique Khan, had spent time at al Qaeda training camps in Afghanistan and had learned bomb-making techniques in Pakistan.

The British public was outraged that four of their own country-men had committed such a deadly attack. But the terrorists' allegiance was to an extremist interpretation of their religion, not to their nation. Two months after the bombings, a previously recorded video of Khan surfaced. On the video, which bore the logo of al Qaeda's media arm,

Khan said, "I and thousands like me are forsaking everything for what we believe. Our driving motivation doesn't come from tangible commodities that this world has to offer." And in one chilling declaration, Khan vowed, "Our words are dead until we give them life with our blood."[64]

Terrorists do shed blood in their quest to achieve political goals. But it is the blood of innocent people toward whom the terrorists show neither compassion nor consideration.

Chapter FIVE

Man-Made Catastrophes

The Great Pyramid at Giza in Egypt is one of the seven wonders of the ancient world. Completed in 2540 BC, the pyramid's blocks fit together with astonishing accuracy, and its alignment to true north and south is remarkable for a people who had no compasses. That the pyramid has stood in the Egyptian desert for more than forty-five hundred years is a testament to the marvels of human engineering.

Not all man-made objects, however, are so enduring. Age and wear and tear limit the useful lives of nearly everything we own. Most houses built today would not last even a few hundred years before deteriorating beyond repair. A twenty-year-old automobile, unless meticulously maintained, would soon be headed for a junkyard. Man-made objects can also fail suddenly with catastrophic results. Sometimes structures weaken over time and reach the point of failure at an inopportune moment: a bridge collapses as people are walking across, or a car's brakes go out on a steep, winding road. At other times people are at fault. Either by recklessness or carelessness, accidents can happen. For example, inattention to a warning signal can put a nuclear power plant, and all those who live nearby, in grave danger. Poor judgment can also turn a serious situation into a disaster. A pilot who tries to fly through a storm instead of around it in order to save a few minutes can find himself in a situation he is not equipped to handle.

Air travel is statistically the safest means of transportation in the world. Airlines fly millions of miles each day without mishap. Yet people build airplanes, people pilot them, and people direct their flight paths from the ground. Despite aviation's outstanding safety record, the possibility for disaster is always lurking in the background.

The Mystery of Flight 447

The Airbus A330 is one of the safest and most advanced passenger airliners in the world. Its sophisticated computer systems can virtually fly the airplane without human input. If there is trouble with airspeed or attitude, the A330 corrects the problem automatically. If a pilot tries to perform a maneuver that would endanger the flight, the computer will prevent that action.

Air France Flight 447, an Airbus A330, took off from Rio de Janeiro, Brazil, on May 31, 2009. Its 228 passengers and crew were headed out over the Atlantic Ocean toward Paris, an eleven-hour trip. Cruising at 35,000 feet (10,668 m), the flight was progressing normally, with the pilots radioing ground controllers in Brazil as they passed various navigation waypoints. At about three hours into the flight, the Airbus approached a waypoint called INTOL. Just beyond this point was a region of intense thunderstorm activity called the Intertropical Convergence Zone. At around 10:35 p.m. one of the pilots acknowledged passing the waypoint to ground controllers; "Air France Four Four Seven, thank you."[65] They were the last words heard from the aircraft.

Into Thin Air

At the next waypoint Flight 447 was supposed to contact controllers in Dakar, Senegal, on the west coast of Africa. But there was no response from the plane to the controller's numerous requests for position confirmation. On flights across the Atlantic Ocean, where aircraft are out of range of land-based radar, radio transmissions are relied upon for flight status. "The fact that they didn't transmit a Mayday," commented William Waldock, a professor of aviation safety, "would seem to indicate that whatever happened to them happened quickly."[66] By all indications, Flight 447 had simply vanished into thin air.

A search-and-rescue force of planes and ships from several nations combed the Atlantic where Flight 447 had made its last transmission. The search came up empty until June 6, when debris was sighted floating on the ocean. Pieces of the aircraft, including the nose and a large piece of the tail fin, were recovered. But the most important objects, the cockpit voice recorder and the flight data recorder—the plane's "black boxes"—remained missing. They were somewhere at the bottom of the Atlantic along with the rest of the plane's wreckage.

Looking for Clues

Without the black boxes, aviation investigators had to rely on the recovered wreckage as their main source of clues. The manner in which an airplane part is damaged can tell investigators a lot about the circumstances surrounding an air disaster. Numerous pieces of wreckage recovered from Flight 447 exhibited an upward deformation, indicating the plane slammed into the water belly first, rather than in a nosedive.

Brazilian military personnel recover debris from the missing Air France Flight 447 that disappeared over the Atlantic Ocean in 2009. Investigators eventually concluded that mechanical failure and a series of human errors contributed to the craft's demise.

The lack of burn marks on the debris and the condition of the recovered bodies were evidence that the aircraft did not explode in midair, ruling out a terrorist bomb or fuel tank explosion.

Investigators also had information that had been automatically sent from the plane. The Aircraft Communications Addressing and Reporting System (ACARS) is a data link between airplanes and the ground that transmits such information as flight conditions, aircraft system status, and maintenance issues. Within three minutes, twenty-four messages from Flight 447 were automatically sent from the plane to the ground. One showed that the aircraft's speed sensors were not working properly. Several messages that the plane's automatic pilot had shut down followed. Other transmissions reported onboard computer problems and abnormal attitude warnings.

The damage on the recovered debris, the ACARS messages, and the known weather on the flight path painted a grim picture of a doomed plane, its instruments knocked out by a thunderstorm, falling out of the sky. Even with all this evidence, however, the conclusion was only an educated guess. Without the black boxes, a definitive answer would never be known.

Discovery on the Ocean Floor

In the two years after the disappearance of Flight 447, Air France and the Airbus Corporation spent $28 million mounting three more search missions. On March 25, 2011, the research ship *Alucia* arrived in the search area. This would be the fourth and final search mission; if the Airbus was not found this time, it and the evidence it held would remain lost forever.

The underwater search was conducted by three autonomous underwater vehicles (AUVs) that are programmed to prowl the ocean floor. On April 2 a sonar image from one of the AUVs showed an object that did not look like a rock or other natural formation. Another submersible was quickly prepared and launched to take photos of whatever was on the bottom. That night, expedition leader Michael Purcell wrote in his journal, "May have found the plane today. Everyone is on edge."[67] The next morning Purcell gathered his team in the *Alucia*'s control room and downloaded the pictures from the second AUV. As they peered intently at a monitor, chilling images soon appeared: a landing gear, a detached jet engine, and a torn portion of fuselage. Air France Flight 447 had been found. Among the items brought up over the next several days were the plane's black boxes. At last the flight data and cockpit conversations during the aircraft's final moments would be revealed.

The Real Story Emerges

As Flight 447 entered the area of the thunderstorm, copilot Pierre-Cédric Bonin advised the cabin crew of turbulence ahead. "In two minutes," Bonin said over the intercom, "we ought to be in an area where it will start moving about a bit [more] than now. You'll have to watch out there."[68] Inexplicably, he did not try to fly the plane around the storm. Within moments things began to go wrong. The plane's automatic pilot suddenly turned off. With this disengaged, the computer no longer prevented the pilots from making dangerous maneuvers. Next, the airspeed indicators malfunctioned, leaving the pilots with no way to know how fast they were flying. "We haven't got a good display of speed,"[69] Bonin commented.

When an aircraft's nose is pointed too far upward, the plane can stall or lose speed and literally fall out of the sky. In the recording, stall warning alarms could clearly be heard, yet the pilots seemed to ignore them. Again, Bonin made an apparently irrational decision and pulled the plane's nose up. The Airbus lost airspeed as it began to climb. More warning chimes sounded as the crew struggled to comprehend their situation. "What's happening? I don't know, I don't know what's happening!"[70] copilot David Robert exclaimed. After two more minutes of trying to bring the plane under control, copilot Bonin cried, "We're going to crash. . . . This can't be true!"[71] Five seconds later, the recording abruptly ended.

Investigators discovered that the airspeed information had disappeared because the plane's speed sensors, called pitot tubes, had iced over as the Airbus flew through the storm. Added to that was the human factor. The final four minutes of Flight 447 must have been extremely stressful for the pilots, and when people are under stress, they make mistakes.

The world may never know why Flight 447 flew into the thunderstorm, or why the pilots ignored the stall warnings. What is known is that mechanical failure and a series of human errors brought Flight 447 to its unfortunate end, destroying a $200 million aircraft and 228 lives.

Disaster at Rush Hour

Disasters can strike without warning, when people going about their everyday routines are suddenly thrust into a potentially life-threatening situation. And few activities are more routine than the daily drive to and from work. The average US commuter drives 16 miles (26 km) to work, and most say they like the convenience of using their own vehicle. Of course, commuting by automobile would not be possible without infrastructure: the streets, expressways, and bridges over which commuters travel. People rely on a safe infrastructure, but it, like anything man-made, is subject to catastrophic failure.

Rush hour in Minneapolis, Minnesota, was at its peak on the evening of August 1, 2007. On the Interstate 35W (I-35W) bridge, an eight-lane steel truss bridge spanning the Mississippi River, cars were moving steadily but slowly. Four lanes had been closed due to construction on the concrete deck of the bridge, bringing traffic to a crawl. Everything had seemed normal until 6:05 p.m., when, without warning, the center span of the bridge gave way. The deck of the bridge, along with 111 vehicles on it, plunged 108 feet (33 m) into the Mississippi River and its banks below. Jay Danz, who was nearby, witnessed the bridge collapse. "I heard it creaking and making all sorts of noises it shouldn't make. And then the bridge just started to fall apart."[72] Sixteen-year-old Leah Fullin had just crossed the bridge when it fell. "Most of the cars that were on the bridge went into the river," she recalled. "There was a whole bunch of smoke when concrete breaks like that. There were people screaming."[73]

Moments after the collapse, the scene was one of chaos. The 456-foot (139 m) center span, the first part of the I-35W bridge to collapse, lay in the water, cars and trucks sitting on the deck as if it were a parking lot. At the east bank of the Mississippi, a huge section of the bridge was thrust upward. On the west bank, cars were strewn like toys on the collapsed end of the bridge. Several vehicles were on fire, sending black smoke into the sky; many cars were submerged in the river. A school bus tipped precariously at one end of the bridge, settling on an angle near a crushed semitrailer. Fortunately, the fifty children aboard the bus were evacuated without major injury.

Catastrophic Failure

"This is a catastrophe of historic proportions for Minnesota,"[74] said Governor Tim Pawlenty shortly after the collapse. A massive search-and-rescue

A horrifying scene awaited rescuers in the aftermath of the catastrophic Interstate 35W bridge collapse in Minnesota in 2007. Investigators blamed a design error as the main cause of the collapse.

effort soon began that included local and state officials, the US Coast Guard, and divers from the FBI and US Navy. About 100 bystanders also helped rescue survivors from mangled vehicles. More than 90 people were rescued from the remains of the bridge, but locating and removing bodies from the wreckage took weeks. When rescue efforts were concluded, statistics confirmed the governor's grim assessment. Thirteen people lost their lives, and 145 were injured. Almost $90 million in settlements would eventually be paid to the victims or their families. In addition, rebuilding the bridge cost $278 million. But the question remained: why had the bridge collapsed?

The National Transportation Safety Board (NTSB), the federal agency tasked with investigating accidents involving all modes of transportation, immediately began an investigation. Their inquiry centered on the design and maintenance of the I-35W bridge. Completed in 1967, the bridge was a truss bridge, built with straight steel beams connected to each other in the shape of large triangles. To form these triangles, steel plates, called gusset plates, join the beams together with rivets, creating structurally strong units. The NTSB discovered that the gusset plates of the I-35W bridge were too thin and gradually had begun to buckle. This process continued slowly over the years, as more traffic and new concrete road surfaces added to the bridge's load. Compared to concrete bridges, steel truss bridges like the I-35W are more vulnerable to wear and tear, according to William Miller, a bridge engineering expert. "Concrete is a very forgiving material," he explained, "and so it can stand up to a lot of cracking and wear. Steel, on the other hand, cannot."[75]

On the day of the collapse, construction vehicles, including two cement trucks weighing 80,000 pounds (36,287 kg) apiece, along with piles of sand and gravel dumped on the bridge, added even more stress to the already weakened gusset plates. As rush hour traffic progressed, one gusset plate finally gave way, causing others to catastrophically fail and ultimately leading to the destruction of the bridge.

Placing Blame

Who was to blame for the I-35W bridge collapse? Fingers pointed in many directions. Eventually, the NTSB concluded that the main cause of the collapse was an error made by the designers of the bridge in the thickness of the gusset plates. The .5 inch (1.3 cm) plates should have been twice as thick in order to support the bridge properly. The Minnesota Department of Transportation (MnDOT) made annual inspections of the bridge, but examining gusset plates was not part of the inspection process. Based on other factors, MnDOT rated the bridge as being structurally deficient and made a recommendation that the bridge be replaced at some time in the future, but there was no sense of urgency to get it done.

America's infrastructure includes hundreds of bridges of the same design as Minneapolis's I-35W bridge. No one knows how many of those are nearing the point of catastrophic failure.

Columbia's Last Flight

When the space shuttle *Columbia* roared off the launching pad on April 12, 1981, it was the beginning of a new era in space exploration for the National Aeronautics and Space Administration (NASA). Unlike older single-use rockets, the shuttle was a reusable vehicle that could fly missions in space and return to Earth to be prepared for another flight. When *Columbia* landed two days after launch, its maiden voyage was hailed as a resounding success. No one could know that twenty-two years later, its last flight would end in disaster.

Columbia's twenty-eighth mission was a sixteen-day scientific research trip. On January 16, 2003, *Columbia* sat on the launch pad at the Kennedy Space Center in Florida attached to two solid rocket boosters and a large external fuel tank. Liftoff at 10:39 a.m. was routine. But eighty-one seconds after launch a piece of foam insulation about the size of a suitcase broke off of the fuel tank and struck the shuttle's left wing. The astronauts were unaware of this, and the shuttle proceeded into orbit to begin its mission.

Critical Decision

On the ground, a debris assessment team of engineers spent days examining high-speed photographs and video of the launch showing the foam breaking away from the tank. But the images did not show the exact location or extent of the damage to the wing. Concerned about the possibility of serious damage, engineers on the team asked flight managers for more photographs to analyze, but they did not receive additional images. The managers ultimately came to the conclusion that the damage caused by the foam did not present a threat to the safety of the shuttle. Halfway through the mission, NASA flight director Steve Stich sent a message to the *Columbia* astronauts. "Experts have reviewed the high-speed photographs and there is no concern for . . . damage. We have seen this phenomenon on several other flights and there is no concern for [re]

Humans Belong in Space

Since Russian Yuri Gagarin became the first human to fly into orbit in 1961, eighteen astronauts and cosmonauts have lost their lives in the conquest of space. *Columbia* was not the first space shuttle to meet a catastrophic end. In 1986 the shuttle *Challenger* exploded seventy-three seconds after liftoff, killing the seven astronauts on board.

Space travel is costly as well. The space shuttle program cost American taxpayers $196 billion. Is space exploration worth the price in dollars and human lives? The answer is yes, according to aerospace engineer Rand Simberg:

> The United States should become a spacefaring nation, and the leader of a spacefaring civilization. That means that access to space should be almost as routine (if not quite as affordable) as access to the oceans, and with similar laws and regulations.
>
> It means that we should have the capability to detect an asteroid or comet heading for Earth and to deflect it in a timely manner. Similarly it means we should be able to mine asteroids or comets for their resources, for use in space or on Earth, potentially opening up new wealth for the planet. It means that we should explore the solar system the way we did the West: not by sending off small teams of government explorers—Lewis and Clark were the extreme exception, not the rule—but by having lots of people wandering around and peering over the next rill [long, narrow valleys on the moon] in search of adventure or profit.

Rand Simberg, "A Space Program for the Rest of Us," *New Atlantis*, Summer 2009. www.thenewatlantis.com.

entry."[76] In fact, the foam had punched a 6- to 10-inch (15- to 25-cm) hole in *Columbia*'s wing. While this had no effect on the operation of the shuttle in space, it would become a fatal flaw during reentry.

"A Blast Furnace"

Once its scientific mission had been completed, the *Columbia* astronauts began preparations for reentry on February 1, 2003. Flying 76 miles

(122 km) over Hawaii, *Columbia* encountered the outer edges of the atmosphere at 8:44 a.m. During this phase of the mission, heat builds up as the shuttle descends, creating a spectacular light show for the astronauts. Looking out *Columbia*'s windows, pilot William McCool commented, "It's really neat, just a bright orange-yellow out over the nose,

PERSPECTIVES

Human Space Travel Is Unnecessary

Humans have been going into space for more than fifty years. Astronauts have walked in space, left footprints on the moon, and built an international space station. But in the twenty-first century, as the cost of spaceflight soared and the economy wavered, many people began asking if it was still worth it to send men and women into space.

Since the early days of the space program, when people gathered around their televisions to watch an astronaut blast off, the launching of space vehicles has become routine. After half a billion people around the world witnessed *Apollo 11* astronaut Neil Armstrong step onto the moon's surface, space missions no longer seem to thrill the imagination.

As a child, theoretical physicist Lawrence M. Krauss dreamed of one day going onto space. Fifty years later, that dream had vanished:

> What happened? Why did the dream of unlimited manned space travel and a vast new universe of possibilities for humanity dry up and fizzle? The answer is relatively simple: reality prevailed. Human space travel is expensive and dangerous, and there is almost no scientific justification for it (a sobering realization for the child-turned-scientist). All these factors stem from the same problem: most of the incredible cost of human space travel goes into keeping humans alive during the process, leaving little money for other things. This harsh reality leaves those of my generation in a position, 50 years hence, of having to reevaluate those childhood dreams.

Lawrence M. Krauss, "Rethinking the Dream of Human Space Flight," *Scientific American*, April 5, 2011. www.scientific american.com.

all around the nose." Mission Commander Rick D. Husband replied, "Looks like a blast furnace."[77]

Space shuttles are designed to withstand this inferno, which can reach 3,000°F (1,649°C). But any damage to the vehicle can provide a pathway for intense heat to enter the structure and quickly destroy vital components. The damage to *Columbia*'s wing caused by the foam strike created just such a pathway. The first indication of trouble came when an officer in Mission Control in Houston, Texas, suddenly lost data from the shuttle. The mechanical systems officer, Jeff Kling, reported, "FYI, I've just lost four separate temperature transducers on the left side of the vehicle."[78] Moments later Kling saw the indications for tire pressure in the landing gear disappear. Tension mounted in Mission Control as word of the malfunctions spread. Controllers watched the large animated map that tracked *Columbia*'s progress, a moving red triangle representing the shuttle flying over Texas. Then, through the speakers, came Husband's voice. "Roger, uh, buh. . . . "[79] The communication abruptly ended. On the map, the triangle had stopped.

The Search for Answers

On the ground in Texas, people watching the shuttle's reentry saw something unexpected. Instead of the single bright trail that signaled the shuttle's appearance, several glowing tracks were arcing through the sky like meteors. They were witnessing the breakup of shuttle *Columbia* as its pieces reentered the atmosphere. Jim Cunningham of Plano watched as the shuttle broke apart. "There were four pieces all flying in formation around the main body of the shuttle just as it went out of view. I thought—well, maybe it's supposed to look like that. When the segments became so large, you knew it wasn't supposed to look like that."[80]

Debris from the *Columbia* was scattered along a line that extended from Texas to Louisiana. For three months more than twenty-five thousand officials and volunteers searched for fragments of the shuttle in fields, farms, and backyards covering an area of 2.3 million acres (930,777 ha). Ultimately, 82,500 pieces of *Columbia* were recovered, weighing some 84,800 pounds (38,465 kg). The pieces were taken to a hangar at the Kennedy Space Center, where they were laid out along a grid to approximate the shape of the shuttle. After a six-month, $400 million investigation, the Columbia Accident Investigation Board published its findings on August 26, 2003. It was confirmed that the primary cause of the *Columbia* disaster was the hole caused by the foam striking the wing, which allowed the heat of reentry to enter the wing and destroy the shuttle. But the board also blamed NASA, where it found a "broken safety culture"[81] in which the dangers of space exploration were downplayed. When NASA engineers voiced concern about the shuttle's foam

Debris from the space shuttle Columbia *streaks across the Texas sky. Although many spectators on the ground did not realize it at first, they were witnessing the breakup of the shuttle as its pieces reentered Earth's atmosphere.*

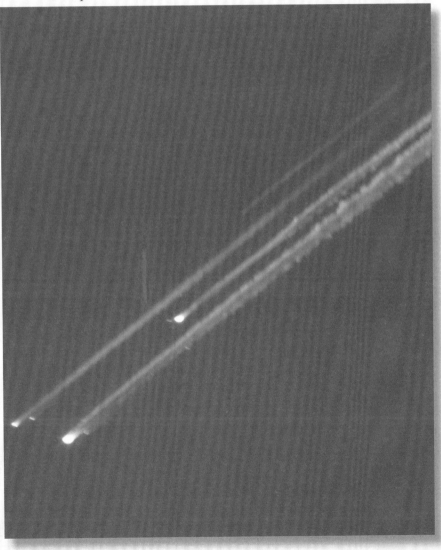

damage, management's lack of concern contributed to the catastrophic failure of space shuttle *Columbia*.

Risks are inherent in any highly technical endeavor, and the space shuttle program was no exception. With an aging shuttle fleet and reduced funding due to a weak economy, NASA ended the space shuttle program in 2011. Its legacy includes thousands of science experiments performed, numerous satellites placed into orbit, and voyages to the International Space Station. And it includes the memory of brave astronauts who accepted the risks in an effort to make a better world for all humankind.

Source Notes

Introduction: A Portent of Catastrophe

1. Quoted in Catherine Winter, "Separating Hype from Reality," *American RadioWorks*. http://americanradioworks.publicradio.org.

Chapter One: Our Restless Earth

2. Quoted in Michael Elliott, "Sea of Sorrow," *Time*, January 10, 2005, p. 31.
3. Quoted in Simon Elegant, "A City of Debris and Corpses," *Time*, January 10, 2005, p. 38.
4. Quoted in Elliott, "Sea of Sorrow," p. 31.
5. Quoted in BBC News, "Eyewitness: Loss and Despair in Aceh." http://news.bbc.co.uk.
6. Quoted in Elegant, "A City of Debris and Corpses," p. 39.
7. Quoted in *Star* (Toronto), "Seven Years Later, Girl Swept Away in Tsunami Reunited with Parents." www.thestar.com.
8. Fuzail Siddiqui, "The South Asian Earthquake of October 8, 2005—an Eyewitness Account," Association of Professional Geoscientists of Ontario. www.apgo.net.
9. Quoted in IRIN Humanitarian News and Analysis, "Pakistan: Earthquake Leaves 20,000 Dead and Huge Numbers in Need." www.irinnews.org.
10. Quoted in Somini Sengupta, "Pakistan Quake Rocks South Asia; over 18,000 Killed," *New York Times*, October 5, 2005. www.nytimes.com.
11. Quoted in IRIN Humanitarian News and Analysis, "Pakistan: Disabled by the 2005 Quake and Still out of School." www.irinnews.org.

12. Quoted in IRIN Humanitarian News and Analysis, "Pakistan: Earthquake Death Toll Likely to Rise Significantly." www.irinnews.org.

13. Quoted in Naomi Lubick, "Kashmir Earthquake," Geotimes. www.geotimes.org.

14. Quoted in Helen Vesperini, "Dozens Die as Lava Enters Congo Town," *The Tribune.* www.tribuneindia.com.

15. Quoted in CNN.com, "Congo Volcano Devastation Mounts," January 18, 2002. www.cnn.com.

16. Quoted in Adrian Blomfield, "Half a Million Flee a River of Molten Rock," *Telegraph* (London). www.telegraph.co.uk.

17. Quoted in Adrian Blomfield, "Lake of Deadly Gas Threatens Fresh Devastation in Goma," *Telegraph* (London). www.telegraph.co.uk.

18. Quoted in Tim Butcher, "Rescue Boats Escape in Water Heated to Boiling Point," *Telegraph* (London). www.telegraph.co.uk.

19. Quoted in Michael Finkel, "The Volcano Next Door," *National Geographic*, April 2011, p. 89.

20. Quoted in Finkel, "The Volcano Next Door," p. 98.

Chapter Two: Killer Weather

21. Quoted in MSNBC.com, "Katrina Forecasters Were Remarkably Accurate." www.msnbc.msn.com.

22. US Department of Commerce, National Oceanic and Atmospheric Administration, National Weather Service, *Service Assessment: Hurricane Katrina, August 23–31, 2005*, Silver Spring, MD, June 2001, p. 18. www.nws.noaa.gov/os/assessments/pdfs/Katrina.pdf.

23. Quoted in Gordon Russell, "Nagin Orders First-Ever Mandatory Evacuation of New Orleans," *New Orleans Times-Picayune*, August 28, 2005. www.nola.com.

24. Quoted in William Hayes, *What Went Wrong: Investigating the Worst Man-Made and Natural Disasters.* New York: Hearst, 2011, p. 104.

25. Quoted in CNN News, *CNN Reports: Katrina—State of Emergency.* Kansas City, MO: Andrews McMeel, 2005, p. 25.

26. Quoted in Editors of *Time* Magazine, *Time: Hurricane Katrina: The Storm That Changed America.* New York: Time Inc. Home Entertainment, 2005, p. 43.

27. Quoted in Amanda Ripley, "How Did This Happen?," *Time*, September 12, 2005, p. 59.

28. Quoted in Ripley, "How Did This Happen?," p. 59.

29. Quoted in Shaoni Bhattacharya, "European Heat Wave Caused 35,000 Deaths," *New Scientist.* www.newscientist.com.

30. Quoted in Frank Bruni, "Europe Sizzles and Suffers in a Summer of Merciless Heat," *New York Times*, August 6, 2003. www.nytimes .com.

31. Quoted in Bruce Crumley, "Elder Careless," *Time,* August 24, 2003. www.time.com.

32. Quoted in Stefan Steinberg, "Thousands Die in European Heat Wave," World Socialist Web Site. www.wsws.org.

33. Quoted in Steinberg, "Thousands Die in European Heat Wave."

34. Quoted in BBC News, "Chirac Promises Health Changes." http:// news.bbc.co.uk.

35. Quoted in Jodi Wilgoren, "Thirty-Nine Left Dead as Tornadoes Shatter Towns," *New York Times,* May 6, 2003. www.nytimes.com.

36. Quoted in Francie Grace, "Worst Week Ever for Twisters," CBS News, February 11, 2009. www.cbsnews.com.

37. Quoted in Wilgoren, "Thirty-Nine Left Dead as Tornadoes Shatter Towns."

38. Quoted in Julie E. Bisbee, "Bush Issues Disaster Declaration After Second Tornado in Two Days Rips Through Oklahoma City," *Brainerd (Minnesota) Dispatch,* May 10, 2003.

Chapter Three: Deadly Diseases

39. Quoted in Donald G. McNeil Jr., "Disease's Pioneer Is Mourned as a Victim," *New York Times*, April 8, 2003. www.nytimes.com.

40. Quoted in McNeil, "Disease's Pioneer Is Mourned as a Victim."

41. World Health Organization, "Global Alert and Response: World Health Organization Issues Emergency Travel Advisory," March 15, 2003. www.who.int.

42. Quoted in Karl Taro Greenfield, *China Syndrome: The True Story of the 21st Century's First Great Epidemic*. New York: HarperCollins, 2006, p. xix.

43. Quoted in Jim Yardley, "After Its Epidemic Arrival, SARS Vanishes," *New York Times*, May 15, 2005. www.nytimes.com.

44. Quoted in CNN.com, "Earliest Case of Swine Flu Tucked Away in Mexico, Officials Say," May 1, 2009. www.cnn.com.

45. Quoted in CNN.com, "More Cases of Swine Flu Reported; WHO Warns of 'Health Emergency,'" www.cnn.com.

46. Quoted in Fox News, "World Health Organization Chief: Swine Flu Outbreak Could Become 'Pandemic,'" April 25, 2009. www.foxnews.com.

47. Quoted in Fox News, "World Health Organization Chief."

48. Margaret Chan, press conference on June 11, 2009. www.who.int/mediacentre/news/statements/2009/h1n1_pandemic_phase 6_20090611/en/index.html.

49. Quoted in Angus Shaw, "No Cholera in Zimbabwe Says Mugabe," *Independent* (London), December 11, 2008. www.independent.co.uk.

50. Quoted in Sebastien Berger and Peta Thornycroft, "Zimbabwe's Cholera Victims 'Ten Times More Likely to Die,'" *Telegraph* (London), December 7, 2008. www.telegraph.co.uk.

51. Richard Sollom, "Zimbabwe's Man-Made Disaster," *Harvard International Review*, July 17, 2009. http://hir.harvard.edu.

Chapter Four: Terrorism Strikes

52. Quoted in Milton Meltzer, *The Day the Sky Fell: A History of Terrorism*. New York: Random House, 2002, p. 69.

53. Quoted in *Huffington Post*, "9/11: How TV Networks Broke the News," video. www.huffingtonpost.com.

54. Quoted in National Commission on Terrorist Attacks, *The 9/11 Commission Report: Final Report of the National Commission on Ter-*

rorist Attacks upon the United States. New York: W.W. Norton, 2004, p. 6.

55. Quoted in National Commission on Terrorist Attacks, *The 9/11 Commission Report*, p. 7.

56. Quoted in Nancy Lee, Lonnie Schlein, and Mitchel Levitas, eds., *A Nation Challenged: A Visual History of 9/11 and Its Aftermath*. New York: *New York Times*, 2002, p. 24.

57. *Washington Post*, "Text: Bush Addresses the Nation on Hijacked Planes," September 11, 2001. www.washingtonpost.com.

58. Quoted in Brian Bennet, "October 12, 2002," *Time*, October 28, 2002. www.time.com.

59. Quoted in Philippa McDonald, "Survivors Recall Horror of Bali Bombing," Australian Broadcasting Corporation News, October 8, 2012. www.abc.net.au.

60. Quoted in BBC News, "Scores Die in Madrid Bomb Carnage," March 11, 2004. http://news.bbc.co.uk.

61. Quoted in BBC News, "Madrid Bombers Get Long Sentences," October 31, 2007. http://news.bbc.co.uk.

62. Quoted in Michael Elliot, "Rush Hour Terror," *Time*, July 10, 2005. www.time.com.

63. Quoted in Alan Cowell, "After Coordinated Bombs, London Is Stunned, Bloodied, and Stoic," *New York Times*, July 7, 2005. www.nytimes.com.

64. Quoted in BBC News, "London Bomber: Text in Full," September 1, 2005. http://news.bbc.co.uk.

Chapter Five: Man-Made Catastrophes

65. Quoted in William Hayes, *What Went Wrong*, p. 137.

66. Quoted in Hayes, *What Went Wrong*, p. 140.

67. Quoted in Wil S. Hylton, "What Happened to Air France Flight 447?," *New York Times Magazine*, May 4, 2011. www.nytimes.com.

68. Quoted in Bureau d'Enquêtes et d'Analyses pour la sécurité de l'aviation civile (BEA), *Flight 447, on 1st June, 2009, A330-203*,

registered F-GZCP, Final Report. Appendix 1, CVR Transcript, p. 21. www.bea.aero/docspa/2009/f-cp090601.en/pdf/annexe.01.en.pdf.

69. Quoted in BEA, *Flight 447, on 1st June, 2009, A330-203, registered F-GZCP, Final Report*, p. 23.

70. Quoted in BEA, *Flight 447, on 1st June, 2009, A330-203, registered F-GZCP, Final Report*, p. 27.

71. Quoted in BEA, *Flight 447, on 1st June, 2009, A330-203, registered F-GZCP, Final Report*, p. 32.

72. Quoted in Paul Levy, "Four Dead, 79 Injured, 20 Missing After Dozens of Vehicles Plummet into River," *Minneapolis Star-Tribune*, August 2, 2007. www.startribune.com.

73. Quoted in Libby Sander and Susan Saulny, "Bridge Collapse in Minneapolis Kills at Least 7," *New York Times*, August 2, 2007. www.nytimes.com.

74. Quoted in Sander and Saulny, "Bridge Collapse in Minneapolis Kills at Least 7."

75. Quoted in Michael D. Lemonick, "Why Did the Bridge Fall?," *Time*, August 2, 2007. www.time.com.

76. Quoted in Michael Cabbage and William Harwood, *Comm Check . . . : The Final Flight of Shuttle Columbia*. New York: Free, 2008, p. 73.

77. Quoted in Cabbage and Harwood, *Comm Check*, p. 9.

78. Quoted in Cabbage and Harwood, *Comm Check*, p. 19.

79. Quoted in Cabbage and Harwood, *Comm Check*, p. 23.

80. Quoted in Kimberly Durnan, "It's Just Horrible," *Dallas Morning News*, February 1, 2003. www.freerepublic.com.

81. Quoted in *Columbia Accident Investigation Board Report*, vol. 1, Washington DC, 2003, p. 184. http://caib.nasa.gov/news/report/pdf/vol1/full/caib_report_volume1.pdf.

Important People: Catastrophic Events of the 2000s

Osama bin Laden: The head of the terrorist group al Qaeda. He masterminded the 9/11 attacks on the World Trade Center and the Pentagon. He was killed by US Navy SEALs on May 2, 2011.

Michael Brown: The head of the Federal Emergency Management Agency. Brown was criticized for his agency's slow response to Hurricane Katrina. He resigned his post on September 12, 2005.

George W. Bush: The president of the United States, 2001–2009. He played key roles in the War on Terror after 9/11 and in the aftermath of Hurricane Katrina.

Margaret Chan: The director general of the World Health Organization since 2006.

Jacques Chirac: The president of France, 1995–2007. He stayed on vacation while his country suffered from a deadly heat wave.

***Columbia* crew:** The seven NASA astronauts who died when the space shuttle *Columbia* broke up on reentry, February 1, 2003: Michael P. Anderson, David M. Brown, Kalpana Chawla, Laurel Clark, Rick D. Husband, William McCool, and Ilan Ramon.

Al Gore Jr.: The vice president of the United States, 1993–2001. After leaving office he became an activist for environmental policy and authored *An Inconvenient Truth: The Planetary Emergency of Global Warming and What We Can Do About It*.

Jiang Yanyong: The physician who leaked information about China's cover-up of the SARS epidemic.

Lee Jong-wook: The director general of the World Health Organization, 2003–2006.

Max Mayfield: The director of the National Hurricane Center, 2000–2007. He warned the mayor of New Orleans of the severity of the approaching Hurricane Katrina.

Robert Mugabe: The president of Zimbabwe. Mugabe is the head of a corrupt regime and denied the existence of cholera in his country.

Ray Nagin: The mayor of New Orleans during Hurricane Katrina. He criticized the government's response to the catastrophe.

Carlo Urbani: The Italian physician who identified the SARS virus. He died of the virus on March 29, 2003.

Words of the 2000s

Note: Below is a sampling of new words or words given new meaning during the decade, taken from a variety of sources.

bailout: Rescue by government of companies on the brink of failure.

birther: A person who believes that Barack Obama was not born in the United States and therefore cannot be president.

bling: Ostentatious displays of fortune and flash.

blog: A weblog.

chad: The tiny paper square that pops out when a voter punches the ballot card while casting a vote.

Chinglish: The growing Chinese-English hybrid language resulting from China's expanding influence.

click-through: Clicking on a banner ad on a website.

cloud computing: The practice of storing regularly used computer data on multiple servers that can be accessed through the Internet.

distracted driving: Multitasking while driving.

frenemy: Someone who is both friend and enemy.

generica: Strip malls, motel chains, prefab housing, and other features of the American landscape that are the same nationwide.

hacktivism: Activism by hackers.

hashtag: The # (hash) symbol used as a tag on Twitter.

helicopter mom/dad: A parent who micromanages his or her children's lives and is perceived to be hovering over every stage of their development.

locavore: Someone who cooks and eats locally grown food.

meh: Boring, apathetic, or unimpressive.

plutoed: To be demoted or devalued, as happened to the former planet Pluto.

push present: An expensive gift given to a woman by her husband in appreciation for having recently given birth.

red state/blue state: States whose residents predominantly vote Republican (red states) or Democrat (blue states).

same-sex marriage: Marriage of gay couples.

sandwich generation: People in their forties or fifties who are caring for young children and elderly parents at the same time.

sexting: Sending of sexually explicit text messages and pictures via cell phones.

snollygoster: A shrewd, unprincipled person; often used to refer to a politician.

staycation: A holiday spent at home and involving day trips to local attractions.

truthiness: Something one wishes to be the truth regardless of the facts.

tweet: To send a message via Twitter.

twixters: Adult men and women who still live with their parents.

unfriend: To remove someone from a friends list on a social networking site such as Facebook.

zombie bank: A financial institution kept alive only through government funding.

Books

Thomas Abraham, *Twenty-First Century Plague: The Story of SARS*. Baltimore: Harper Perennial, 2007.

Douglas Brinkley, *The Great Deluge: Hurricane Katrina, New Orleans, and the Mississippi Gulf Coast*. New York: William Morrow, 2007.

Michael Cabbage and William Harwood, *Comm Check . . . : The Final Flight of Shuttle Columbia*. New York: Free, 2008.

James R. Chiles, *Inviting Disaster: Lessons from the Edge of Technology: An Inside Look at Catastrophes and Why They Happen*. New York: Harper Business, 2002.

Herbert Genzmer, Sybille Kershner, and Christian Schutz, *Great Disasters: Natural and Manmade Catastrophes That Have Changed the World*. Bath, UK: Parragon, 2010.

William Hayes, *What Went Wrong: Investigating the Worst Man-Made and Natural Disasters*. New York: Hearst Communications, 2011.

Robert Kovach and Bill McGuire, *The Firefly Guide to Global Hazards*. Buffalo, NY: Firefly, 2004.

Barry LePatner, *Too Big to Fall: America's Failing Infrastructure and the Way Forward*. New York: Foster, 2010.

David Quammen, *Spillover: Animal Infections and the Next Human Pandemic*. New York: W.W. Norton, 2012.

David Robson, *The Decade of the 2000s*. San Diego: ReferencePoint, 2012.

Websites

Centers for Disease Control and Prevention, "Natural Disasters and Severe Weather" (http://emergency.cdc.gov/disasters/). Provides information on emergency preparedness and other topics related to natural disasters.

FBI, "Terrorism" (www.fbi.gov/about-us/investigate/terrorism). Provides information on terrorist threats, precautions, intelligence operations, monitoring, and other FBI activities.

National Academy of Engineering, "Transportation Infrastructure" (www.nae.edu/Publications/Bridge/TransportationInfrastructure .aspx). Provides links to reports on the safety of bridges and other aspects of transportation infrastructure.

National Geographic, "Natural Disasters" (http://environment.nat ionalgeographic.com/environment/natural-disasters/). This website has articles, photos, and videos of every kind of natural disaster, from avalanches to wildfires.

World Health Organization, "Global Alert and Response" (www .who.int/csr/outbreaknetwork/en/). This website has information on infectious diseases and how WHO and other public health agencies respond to possible pandemics.

*Note: Boldface page numbers
indicate illustrations.*

Afghanistan
  al Qaeda in, 56
  British terrorists in, 61
  radical Islamists suicide attacks
    (2000–2004), 50
aftershocks following earthquakes, 18–19
AIDS, 44
Airbus A330, 64–67, **65**
aircraft accidents
  Air France Flight 447, 64–67, **65**
  Columbia space shuttle, 71–76, **75**
Aircraft Communications Addressing
  and Reporting System (ACARS), 66
Air France Flight 447 (2009) accident,
  64–67, **65**
air travel safety record, 63
Alaska
  earthquake drills, 17
  earthquakes in, 14
  tsunami, 14
Aleutian Islands, Alaska, 14
Alexander II (tsar of Russia), 50
Allen, Mike, 33
al Qaeda
  London attacks, 61–62
  Madrid attacks, 59
  September 11 attacks, 54
  War on Terror, 56
Alucia (research ship), 66
American Airlines Flight 11, 51–52
American Airlines Flight 77, 52
American Civil Liberties Union, 55
anticyclones, 30
Apollo 11 space craft, 73
Arkansas, tornadoes in, 32, 33
Armstrong, Neil, 73
autonomous underwater vehicles
  (AUVs), 66

Bahamas and Katrina, 24
Bali, terrorist attacks in, 56–58
Banda Aceh, Sumatra, 11–15
Beirne, Chris, 57
Biello, Mark, 26
bin Laden, Osama, 56
bin Nurhasyim, Amrozi, 57
blue death, 46–49
Bonin, Pierre-Cédric, 67
Botswana, 49
bridge collapse (2007), Minnesota,
  68–71, **69**
Brown, Michael, 27–28
Brundtland, Gro Harlem, 37
Buras, Louisiana, 25
Burma (tectonic) plate, 12
Bush, George W.
  Katrina hurricane, 26
  Patriot Act, 54
  2003 tornadoes, 34, 35
  War on Terror, 56
Bustami, 12, 13

California, earthquake drills in, 17
Cameroon (1986) gases release, 21
Canada
  earthquake drills in, 17
  SARS in, 40, 41
carbon dioxide, 21, 28
Centers for Disease Control and
  Prevention (CDC), 42, 45
Challenger space shuttle, 72
Chan, Margaret, 44, 45
China
  SARS in, 37, 38–41, **39**
  swine flu in, 42
Chirac, Jacques, 32
cholera (2008) outbreak
  cause, 46, **47**, 48
  cure, 46–48
  fighting, 48–49

climate change, 28
Colorado, tornadoes in, 32, 33
Columbia space shuttle (2003 flight)
  destruction, 74–76, **75**
  liftoff damage, 71–72
  reentry, 72–74
Colvolino, Stefano, 30–31
computers, potential crisis, 8–10
Córdova, José angel, 42
coronaviruses, 38
Couric, Katie. *See* September 11, 2001,
  attacks
Cuba, swine flu in, 42
Cullen, George, 35
Cunningham, Jim, 74

Danz, Jay, 68
deaths
  Alaska tsunami, 14
  Bali attack, 57
  cholera, 46, 48, 49
  crash of Air France Flight 447, 67
  European heat wave, 30, 31–32
  gases release in Cameroon, 21
  Indian Ocean tsunami, 15
  Kashmir earthquake, 16–17, 19
  Katrina hurricane, 26, 28
  London terrorist attacks, 61
  Madrid terrorist attacks, 59, **60**
  Minnesota bridge collapse, 69
  radical Islamist suicide attacks
    (2000–2004), 50
  SARS, 38, 41
  September 11, 2001, attacks, 50, 51, 54
  Spanish flu, 36
  swine flu epidemic, 42, 45
  Tornado Alley 2003 twisters, 33
dehydration, 46
Democratic Republic of Congo (2002)
  volcano eruption, 19–22, **20**
diabetes, 40
diet and disease, 40
diseases
  cholera, 46–49, **47**
  diabetes, 40
  HIV/AIDS, 44
  SARS, 37–41, **39**
  Spanish flu, 36

swine flu (H1N1 virus), 42–46, **43**
Doctors Without Borders, 48
drinking water, 46, **47**, 48

Earth Policy Institute, 30
earthquake drills, 17
earthquakes
  aftershocks, 18–19
  Alaska, 14
  beneath oceans, 11
  India, 17
  Kashmir, 16–19
  overview of, 11
earth's layers, 11
Egypt, 63
El Niño, 30
El Niño Cero ("Little Boy Zero") statue,
  45–46
England, (2005) terrorist attacks in, 59,
  61–62
Ernest N. Morial Convention Center,
  Louisiana, 26
Europe
  heat wave, 30–32
  London terrorist attacks, 59, 61–62
  Madrid terrorist attacks, 58–59, **60**
evacuation in New Orleans, 25

Federal Emergency Management Agency
  (FEMA), 27–28
Feinstein, Diane, 54
Finland, swine flu in, 42
fissure volcanic eruptions, 19
Florida and Katrina, 24
Fujita scale, 33
Fullin, Leah, 68

Gardner, Jasmine, 61
gases release (1986) in Cameroon, 21
gene reassortment, 42
GeoHazards International/Society of
  India, 17
Georgia Institute of Technology, 28
global warming and weather patterns,
  28, 29
Goma (2002) volcano eruption,
  Democratic Republic of Congo,
  19–22, **20**

Gore, Al, Jr., 28
Great Pyramid at Giza, Egypt, 63
Ground Zero. *See* September 11, 2001,
  attacks
Guangdong, China, SARS in, 38
gusset plates, 70

Hall, Julie, 41
Hanson, Peter, 52
Hartl, Gregory, 42
Hawaii, (1946) tsunami, 14
heat waves, 30–32
Hernandez, Edgar, 42, 45–46
Hicks, Michael, 50
HIV/AIDS, 44
H1N1 virus. *See* swine flu (2009)
  epidemic
Hong Kong, SARS in, 37, 39, 41
Hooper-Box, Caroline, 48
hurricanes
  Katrina
    beginning of, 24
    effects of, 25–29, **27**
    warning about, 24
  measuring, 24
  occurrence of severe, 28, 29
Husband, Rick D., 74

Illinois, tornadoes in, 32, 33
India
  earthquake drills, 17
  Kangra Valley earthquake, 17
  Kashmir and, 16–19
India (tectonic) plate, 12
Indonesia, **13**, 37, 56–58
influenza
  Spanish flu, 36, 42
  swine flu, 41–46, **43**
International Committee of the Red
  Cross, 48
Intertropical Convergence Zone, 64
INTOL waypoint, 64
Iowa, tornadoes in, 32, 33
Iraq, 50, 56

Japan, earthquake drills in, 17
Jemaah Islamiyah, 57
Jiang Yanyong, 41

Johns, Hattie, 25

Kansas, tornadoes in, 32, 33
Kashmir earthquake (2005), 16–19
Katrina (2005) hurricane
  beginning of, 24
  effects of, 25–29, **27**
  warning about, 24
Khan, Ali, 18
Khan, Jawad, 17–18
Khan, Mohammad Sidique, 61–62
Kling, Jeff, 74
Krauss, Lawrence M., 73

La Gloria, Mexico, 41–42, 45–46
Lake Kivu, Democratic Republic of
  Congo, 21
Lake Pontchartrain, Louisiana, 23, 25
landslides, 18–19, 31
Lindsay, Germaine, 59, 61
London, England (2005) terrorist
  attacks, 59, 61–62
Louisiana Superdome, 25–26
Lowry, Chris, 59, 61

Macloed, Andrew, 16
Madrid, Spain (2004) terrorist attacks,
  58–59, **60**
Mayfield, Max, 24, 29
McCool, William, 73–74
meteorological predictions, 23
methane release (1986) in Cameroon, 21
Mexico, swine flu in, 41–46, **43**
Mexico City, Mexico, 43–44, **43**
Millennium Bug, 8–10
Miller, William, 70
Minneapolis, Minnesota (2007) bridge
  collapse, 68–71, **69**
Minnesota
  Mississippi River bridge collapse in,
    68–71, **69**
  tornado in, **34**
Missouri, tornadoes in, 32, 33
moment magnitude scale, 11
Mount Nyiragongo (2002) volcano
  eruption, 19–22, **20**
Mozambique, 49
Mugabe, Robert, 46, 48

Muzaffarabad, Kashmir, 16–19

Nagin, Ray
  evacuation order issued by, 24–25
  on federal government response to
    Katrina, 26–27
  warned about Katrina, 24
National Aeronautics and Space
    Administration (NASA)
  "broken safety culture," 75–76
  Columbia space shuttle, first flight, 71
  Columbia space shuttle, 2003 flight
    destruction, 74–76, **75**
    liftoff damage, 71–72
    reentry, 72–74
National Center for Atmospheric
    Research, 28
National Transportation Safety Board
    (NTSB), 70
Nature (journal), 28
Nebraska, tornadoes in, 32
New Orleans, Louisiana
  Katrina and
    beginning of, 24
    effects of, 25–29, **27**
    warning about, 24
  location of, 23, 24–25
New Zealand, 17, 42
Noinville, Paule de, 31
Novotny, Thomas, 40

Obama, Barack, 42
Oklahoma, tornadoes in, 32, 33–34
Oregon, earthquake drills in, 17
Ortiz, Roberto, 44

Pacific Tsunami Warning Center
    (PTWC), 14
Pakistan
  British terrorists in, 61
  Kashmir and, 16–19
  radical Islamists suicide attacks
    (2000–2004), 50
Paradela, Antonia, 13–14
Pasha, Riffat, 16–17
Patriot Act (US, 2001), 54, 55
Pawlenty, Tim, 68
Pelloux, Patrick, 31

Pentagon. *See* September 11, 2001,
    attacks
Philippines, SARS in, 37
Phuket, Thailand, 15
Pierce City, Missouri, 33
pitot tubes, 67
pneumonia. *See* Severe Acute Respiratory
    Syndrome (SARS)
Presa, Isabel, 59
Purcell, Michael, 66

radical Islamist terrorist attacks
  in Bali, 56–58
  deaths from (2000–2004), 50
  in London, 59, 61–62
  in Madrid, 58–59, **60**
  See also September 11, 2001, attacks
reassortment of genes, 42
Red Cross (International), 48
rehydration, 46–47, 49
Reingold, Barry, 55
Richter scale, 11
Rizal, Isnie, 12, 14–15
Robert, David, 67
Rohde, David, 52

Saffir-Simpson scale, 24
Schuchat, Anne, 42
September 11, 2001, attacks
  described, 51–53, **53**
  effects
    deaths, 54
    destruction, 55
    economic costs, 55–56
    Patriot Act, 54, 55
    TSA established, 50
    War on Terror, 56
  terrorists involved, 54
Severe Acute Respiratory Syndrome
    (SARS)
  containment, 41
  deaths from, 38, 41
  effects, 39–40
  outbreak and spread of, 37–38, **39**
ShakeOut earthquake drills, 17
Shanksville, Pennsylvania, 52
Siddiqui, Fuzail, 16
silent killer (diabetes), 40

Simberg, Rand, 72
Singapore, SARS in, 37
Sollom, Richard, 48
Somalia, 15
South Africa, 48, 49
space flight
    Columbia space shuttle (2003) flight,
        71–76, **75**
    cost, 72
    further human travel is unnecessary, 73
    history, 72, 73
    humans belong in space, 72
Spain, 2004 terrorist attacks in, 58–59,
    60
Spanish flu, 36, 42
Sri Lanka, 15
Stich, Steve, 71–72
storm surges, 25
suicide bombers. *See* terrorism
Sultan, Shaukat, 18
Sumatra, 11–15
Superdome, Louisiana, 25–26
swine flu (2009) epidemic
    cause of, 41–42
    effects of, 42, 44, 45–46
    precautions against, 43–44, **43**
    spread of, 42
    vaccine to combat, 45
Synolakis, Costas, 14

Taiwan, SARS in, 41
tectonic plates, 11, 12, 16
Tedesco, Dario, 22
Tennessee, tornadoes in, 33
terrorism
    assassination of tsar of Russia, 50
    Bali attack, 56–58
    deaths from radical Islamist suicide
        attacks (2000–2004), 50
    London attacks, 59, 61–62
    Madrid attacks, 58–59, **60**
    See also September 11, 2001, attacks
Texas, tornadoes in, 32
Thailand
    SARS in, 37
    swine flu in, 42
    tsunami and, 15
thunderstorms and aircraft, 64, 66

Tornado Alley, 32–35, **34**
tornadoes
    average yearly number of, 32–33
    fictional, 23
    formation of, 32
    measuring, 33
    in 2003 in Tornado Alley, 33, 34, **34**,
        35
Transportation Security Administration
    (TSA), 50
Tropical Depression 12, 24
    See also Katrina (2005) hurricane
tsunamis
    Alaska, 14
    cause of, 11
    Hawaii, 14
    Indian Ocean
        cause, 11–12
        described, 12–13
        effects of, 13–16, **13**
        warning of, 14
    warning system for, 14
Tucker, Brian, 18
Twin Towers, New York City. *See*
    September 11, 2001, attacks
twisters. *See* tornadoes

United Airlines Flight 93, 52
United Airlines Flight 175, 51, 52, **53**
United States
    cost of space shuttle program, 72
    earthquake drills in, 17
    effect of SARS in, 40
    First and Fourth Amendments to
        Constitution, 55
    swine flu national emergency, 42
    swine flu vaccine, 45
    TSA established, 50
    See also September 11, 2001, attacks;
        specific catastrophes
Urbani, Carlo, 36–37, 38
USA Patriot Act (2001), 54, 55

Vibrio cholerae, 46
Virunga National Park volcano eruption,
    Democratic Republic of Congo,
    19–22, **20**
volcanoes, 19–22, **20**

Waldock, William, 64
Wall Street Journal (newspaper), 14
War on Terror, 56
Washington, earthquake drills in, 17
Wati, 15–16
weather
  carbon dioxide releases and, 28
  human activity and, 28, 29
  natural cycles to, 29
  thunderstorms, 64, 66
  See also hurricanes; tornadoes
Wilson, George, 35

Wizard of Oz, The (film), 23
World Food Programme (UN), 15
World Health Organization (WHO), 37, 44
World Trade Center, New York City. *See* September 11, 2001, attacks

Yangzom, 17
Y2K (Year 2000) Bug, 8–10
Yuranda, Meri, 13, 16

Zambia, 49
Zimbabwe, 46, 47–48, **47**, 49

Picture Credits

Cover: Thinkstock Images

AP Images: 13, 20, 39, 43, 47, 53, 60, 65, 69, 75

Timothy A. Clary/AFP/Newscom: 9

Science Photo Library: 34

Thinkstock Images: 6, 7

US Air Force/Science Faction/Corbis: 27

Craig E. Blohm has written numerous books and magazine articles for young readers. He and his wife, Desiree, reside in Tinley Park, Illinois.

WOODLAND HIGH SCHOOL
800 N. MOSELEY DRIVE
STOCKBRIDGE, GA 30281
(770) 389-2784